THE SUICIDE KIT

Born in West Sussex in 1970, David L. Hayles studied film and theatre at London University. After a year in the Caribbean working as a cocktail waiter, he returned to London to study journalism. He has since worked for MTV and the BBC.

David L. Hayles

THE SUICIDE KIT

V

VINTAGE

Published by Vintage 2003

2 4 6 8 10 9 7 5 3 1

Copyright © David L. Hayles, 2002

First published in Great Britain in 2002 by
Secker & Warburg

Vintage
Random House, 20 Vauxhall Bridge Road,
London SW1V 2SA

Random House Australia (Pty) Limited
20 Alfred Street, Milsons Point, Sydney
New South Wales 2061, Australia

Random House New Zealand Limited
18 Poland Road, Glenfield,
Auckland 10, New Zealand

Random House (Pty) Limited
Endulini, 5A Jubilee Road, Parktown 2193,
South Africa

The Random House Group Limited Reg. No. 954009
www.randomhouse.co.uk

A CIP catalogue record for this book
is available from the British Library

ISBN 0 09 943182 3

Papers used by Random House are natural, recyclable
products made from wood grown in sustainable forests.
The manufacturing processes conform to the environ-
mental regulations of the country of origin

Printed and bound in Great Britain by
Bookmarque Ltd, Croydon, Surrey

To C. T. R. Phillips,
the one, the only

E. Z. Helm, who was
there at the beginning

And Victoria de Lotz,
without whom...

Dedicated to
Warren Zevon

contents

the typing pool

A man, elegantly dressed in a tweed suit, a waistcoat and a white shirt with starched collar and cuffs, stood at the end of a small assembly hall; in front of him were five rows, five desks across, each desk with a typewriter and a stack of paper upon it. With the exception of a nervous-looking man in the fifth row, at the back on the right-hand side, all those seated were women – young, in their twenties, and well presented. They sat attentively, waiting for the man in the suit to speak.

Instead, he paced back and forth in front of them, occasionally turning to fix one of the girls with his gaze. None of them dared think anything unpleasant about him. He looked like the type to read minds. None of them except Helen Blackworth, a 26-year-old, sat in the third row of the hall, who thought, the pompous bastard, he must have used all the butter in the camp to get his hair that slick.

'You are here on account of your typing speeds,' he began. 'Your records show speeds ranging from eighty to one hundred and ten words a minute. These are quite exemplary speeds. Today will be a test of those speeds. For the position that is to be filled, you will need to achieve in excess of eighty words per minute. Anything less than that will be useless to me.' He had begun to accelerate his words as if to illustrate that point. 'Now, if any of you have put down, say, eighty, when the truth is closer to fifty-five or sixty, in the hope of attaining the position, it is quite pointless. It will be a complete waste of everybody's time, and will count badly against you.' As he said this, his words full of dark threat and suggestion, the man sitting at the back of the hall cried out, leaped up kicking his chair away, and ran to the exit. The women sat and listened to his footsteps clatter across the concrete outside. A few moments later there was a bark of gunfire. The footsteps halted and the man cried out again.

'We will begin the test,' the man in the suit continued, unperturbed by the disturbance. 'Of the twenty . . . four of you, only one will be successful. The others – well, good luck.'

The man in the suit began his dictation and twenty-four typewriters rattled into life. The man's speech was fast and well rehearsed; it was a deliberately vicious, provocative and hateful treatise, and he relished every foul moment of it, only slowing to roll his R's.

At first, the women typed away diligently, their heads bowed towards the white sheets of paper being dragged and shaken into the roller of each machine and emerging dirtied with grotesque sentences. But soon, as specks of foam began to appear at the corners of the man's mouth, and he began to roll his eyes and gesticulate, and the speech filled with bile, some of the women lost words, then phrases and sentences as they looked up to see if he really had just said what they'd heard. His face, the muscles constricted and the veins bulging in his neck, were testament that he had. One woman stood up and cried out, 'I CAN'T STAND IT!' and some of the other women nodded, hoping it might lead to a reprieve.

The man interrupted himself just once to say, quite calmly, 'Sit down. You have no choice. You know the alternative.'

The woman shoved the typewriter defiantly off the desk and started out of the hall, and he recommenced the dictation. The rattle of the typewriters drowned out the crackle of gunfire outside that followed seconds after.

Helen Blackworth believed that luck was on her side that day. The typewriter – an Olympian Ampersand, identical to all the others in the room – was the very model she had learned to type on, and the one she'd used every day since. It was a cinch for her to hit one hundred words a minute, even more so when the man lent certain words undue pronunciation to stress their vulgarity, a tactic deliberately deployed to put the girls off their keystroke. But Helen had heard it all before. She'd worked for her father. *He'd* liked to write letters to the newspapers. He'd got into a lot of trouble for *that*.

Helen's fingers danced over the keyboard. Occasionally she would reach and grab a full sheet of paper out of the roller like she was pulling the guts out of a fish, and feed a new sheet in.

It doesn't matter how long this goes on, she thought, because I can keep up with him.

The girl next to her screamed and ran from her desk. Helen typed on.

By the amount of ribbon left on the spool, Helen estimated she could type only four more pages. If he spoke for more than ten minutes, they'd all be sunk, because they hadn't been supplied with an extra ribbon, and the ribbons on the Ampersand were non-reversible. Only four typists remained.

It felt like he would carry on for as long as there was air for him to breathe. He'd gone off on a depraved tangent now, digressing into a lurid sexual fantasy that he was using as a political metaphor. Of the four remaining, only one would survive. Helen knew that; no-one in that room, after hearing what they had heard, could be allowed to survive, unless they were in the employ of the state, and were obliged to be discreet. Callous as it sounded, Helen knew she would survive. No-one else remained of her family. If she went, the Blackworth name would be consigned to the earth.

She knew she couldn't let that happen, and she was strong enough not to allow it to happen. She hadn't been born strong, she had learned it, like one learns anything. But it had taken years, and it was an ongoing learning process, perhaps the only one that never ceased.

One page was left and he was still in full flow. He had thrown off his jacket now and was pacing the hall bellowing to the ceiling as if he was giving an operatic performance.

Of the four, Helen was the only one who sat upright and maintained a steady speed on the typewriter keyboard. The others faltered, and, terrified, began to show signs of wear and tear.

'And this,' he cried out, 'is what you were put on this earth for! This is your purpose! Full point. New paragraph.'

Helen's wrists began to ache. I hope he finishes soon, she thought, *for the others' sakes* . . .

She looked at the ribbon.

There was half a page, maximum.

One of the girls fell forward at her desk and sobbed.

Helen felt her hands seizing up. When he caught his breath she took the opportunity to flex her fingers, then resumed.

Another woman's hands had seized up, and she sat bewildered, staring at the frozen digits which had forced a clump of metal hammers out all at once, jamming them uselessly on to the same place on the page.

There were two of them left now.

Only sentences left.

They typed on.

He showed no signs of finishing.

Helen watched as the typewriter ribbon came loose from the left-hand spool and was dragged across to the right and passed across her in the middle, as he

Proceeding in his normal morning routine, Earle Griffin performed twenty star jumps, showered and then dressed, putting on a freshly laundered shirt with starched collar and cuffs, a blue tie and silver cufflinks, his best tweed suit and black leather shoes.

Today he had assembled twenty-five candidates for his dictation. It was long and complicated and contained many difficult words and, furthermore, he knew people would find it outrageous. That was partly the point. Of the twenty-five, one was a man who, Griffin knew, had lied about his typing speeds, but Griffin had selected him for the sport of it.

Griffin stood in front of the mirror, slicking back his hair with a silver metal comb.

'You devil,' he said to himself, and smirked.

Today, he knew, would be a fine day.

Griffin had no need to employ a secretary to take dictation. He rarely sent letters, preferring instead to speak with people over the telephone. But the budget allowed the position, and Middleman was keen he should fill it, lest the budget for the camp be cut back the next year if they didn't make full use of it. They could always reallocate the funds in the future, but in the meantime it would do well to keep the position filled.

Middleman had come up with the idea of filling the post from within the camp, which Griffin immediately seized upon as an excellent idea. 'Make use of the good-for-nothings,' he said.

The assembly hall smelled of floor polish. The floorboards creaked under his feet as Griffin walked between the desks to the far end of the hall. Everyone was seated when he arrived. He could sense their terror. They'd seen the riflemen outside.

He looked at the women. They tried to appear calm as best they could.

They should be worried, he thought. Griffin had prepared the speech with extraordinary precision. Why not? What else was there for him to do with his time? He'd had Middleman's assistant type it up and tailored it so that the speech used an entire length of typewriter ribbon. It would add some tension to the thing – if the typists misspelt a word, or crossed out one to retype it, they would certainly lose the end of the speech. If they missed out words, there would be ribbon left, and that would be telling also. Perhaps one would produce the perfect manuscript that would match, page breaks and all, the prototype manuscript Middleman's assistant had prepared, that he would read from today.

Middleman's assistant had typed and retyped the speech as they fitted it to the correct length, and it amused Griffin to see her initial reaction of shock, and revulsion, soon turn to casual acceptance. By the end of the task she didn't even bat an eyelid. Given time, people would always be tolerant, he felt. Griffin unfolded the speech. The typists' hands were poised over their keyboards.

He began.

'Full point. Ends,' Griffin said, and let out a breath.

Helen stared down dumbfounded. The final full point would be the last thing that ribbon ever printed. If that wasn't luck being on her side today, nothing was! She took the sheet of paper out of the roller and laid it face down on the stack, which she turned over and patted the sides until all the pages were neatly together. It was as if she had been in a trance all that time, which she was now slowly coming out of. She looked over at the other woman, who had not yet taken the final sheet of paper out of her machine. Instead, the woman stood, wearily pushing back her chair, then turned and began a slow walk to the doors.

'Don't,' Helen called out, as the woman went outside.

Helen tensed, then slouched after the gunfire rang out.

'Well then,' Griffin said, approaching her desk. 'Let's see how you did.'

After only a couple of days in her new job, Helen realised she would not be required to do much at all, apart from sit in Griffin's office, and note down the occasional call for him when he was not there, which was most of the time.

That all those others had died, and had been put through that, for *this* . . . she found quite bewildering, and she sat feeling numbed by the dullness and hopelessness of it all.

When she did see Griffin, with his smart suits and slick hair, she asked him if there was something she might do, and he seemed to think he was doing her a favour by telling her there wasn't. Worse than that, Griffin was a fair employer, and he tried to be charming and accommodate Helen, and flattered her with compliments, allowed her time off, and wouldn't think of burdening her with work. He was always well presented and made persistent offers of dinner dates that would get her out of the camp and into elegant surroundings.

She was not in the least bit tempted by any of this; it made no impact on her. She politely declined, saying they should keep their relationship on a professional basis. Of course, this was out of the question. It could never be professional, and Helen knew that. He held her fate in his hand, and because of that she was linked to Earle Griffin until one of them, or both of them, died. At times she wondered who was the lucky one of the twenty-five.

Griffin could not understand Helen's reluctance to accept

his invitations to dinner, to the music, to the wine. He had the best cellar on the camp, anyone knew that, he wasn't much older than her, he was well dressed, he held a position of power; he was quite handsome and had a rogueish quality – in short, he had everything going for him. These were things that should intoxicate a woman!

Despite his persistence, his requests were greeted with the same blank reticence. It began to upset and annoy him. And all the time she would ask for work.

Of the twenty-five, he'd chosen the one more interested in working than living!

It was Wednesday morning, and Griffin decided to call into the office before going on his rounds.

He went in and Helen was sat at her desk in front of the typewriter.

'Is there anything you'd like me to do this morning?' she asked him.

'Nothing for you to do. Lucky for some. I have a very busy morning ahead. Some of the prisoners have got up on the roof of one of the blocks, and Middleman has asked me to organise the riflemen to get them down.'

Helen felt her stomach lurch. She steadied herself. 'You don't understand,' she said. 'I would like to do something. Is there something you would like me to type?'

He leaned forward so that she could smell his hair

pomade, which smelled of wood polish. 'You type whatever you like,' he told her, then brushed her chin with his forefinger, and left the office.

What was I thinking of? Griffin thought as he went on his way. I really should have given the girl something to do. What else was she doing there? I'd had big plans for that girl, he thought, to degrade her verbally. That was before he'd *fallen* for her. His plans had rather gone off the boil since. He should put his mind to a dictation. No use letting her sit idle. He would think of something.

The head rifleman approached him when he reached the block where the prisoners had got up on the roof.

Griffin looked up at the roof but the sun blazed across its surface so he couldn't see anyone up there.

'They've issued a complaint,' the rifleman told him.

'They don't have any rights.'

'It's about Christmas dinner.'

'Damn! We organise something nice, and this is how they react. I suppose they are demanding a particular wine to go with the meal.'

'They say they shouldn't have to attend.'

'Of course they must attend. Everyone will be there.'

'They don't celebrate Christmas.'

'They will this year.'

'They are adamant, sir.'

'Get them down.'

'How?'

Griffin looked at the head rifleman as if it was the most stupid question he'd ever been asked. The rifleman nodded and went back to his men.

A few days later Helen knocked on Middleman's door, and was admitted.

'What can I do for you, Miss Blackworth?' Middleman asked her.

'It's Mr Griffin,' she said.

'What about him? Has he been mistreating you? There's nothing I can do about that, I'm afraid.'

'Not at all. He's very good to me. It's just – I don't like to . . .' She paused and gripped the manuscript in her left hand. 'This,' she said, and thrust the manuscript forward.

Middleman took it and perused it.

'Oh dear,' he said, and set the manuscript on the desk. 'He has been acting rather strangely,' Middleman went on. 'And the business with the prisoners the other day as well. This is most upsetting.'

'What will happen?'

'He'll have to go. And I'm afraid you'll have to go also.'

Helen bowed her head. 'I didn't want to . . .'

'There was nothing you could do. You were right to come here.'

*

Earle Griffin did twenty star jumps, showered and dressed. He was to face the riflemen at eleven that morning, and he wanted to look good. They'd done the girl the day before, and he hadn't been able to convince anyone that she was lying, that she'd written that thing. That he'd had nothing to do with it.

He looked at himself in the mirror. Don't think you won't die at the hands of a woman, he thought. He combed back his hair, and said, 'You're going to die you devil, you're dead.'

the suicide kit

Thousands of people commit suicide every year. The figures are rising. We can blame this on many factors, but the causes are too numerous to go into here. The simple fact is, people will commit suicide, so what options are open to them?

The rope noose, the car exhaust, a shotgun in the mouth, the oven, pills, razor blades, the leap, the tube train, the speeding truck, the railway tracks, the river, canal or pond, an electrical appliance in the bath, two pencils in the nostrils at exam time, ether, strychnine, rat poison, toxic gas? Forget about it!

The Suicide Kit provides a clean, fast suicide that will let you go out not only with dignity, but without adding to what you're already suffering. With The Suicide Kit, your body will remain more or less intact. You won't have to worry about your wife finding your brains on the living room wall, or a young couple on a moonlit night coming across your bloated corpse on the riverbank, or a train driver pulling your headless torso out from under the wheels of his train. Relatives won't have to attend your funeral knowing the coffin contains your mangled body, the result of a thirteen-floor jump before you exploded like an overripe melon on the pavement below.

The Suicide Kit is 100% guaranteed. Your money back, and another kit, free of charge, if you don't receive satisfaction.

So, go out the way you want to go:

> **The Suicide Kit**
> No pills, no guns, no bloody mess.
> Credit cards accepted.
> Senior citizen discounts.
> Cults – we do special offers on bulk orders.

the dwarf-wrangler

'Looking at your CV, your last job — did it involve a regular three-pronged trident or the cat-o'-nine-tails?'

'Trident. Cat-o'-nine-tails is good for crowd control, but for individual attention it has to be the trident.'

'Were the dwarves caged or chained?'

'Caged. We had them caged since the shortage of dwarf manacles back in '12.'

'Mmm. How many dwarves?'

'Thirty.'

'In one cage — is that legal?'

'You can have up to sixty. Depends on the size of the cage.'

'Did you ever have any trouble with the dwarves, Mr Gants?'

'Mr Jenkins, with all due respect, I've had six years

experience of dwarf-wrangling. I don't let the midgets bother me.'

'Especially if you are holding a three-pronged trident, eh?'

'There was one dwarf. You can tell the troublemakers. While all the other dwarves are trying to shake the cage, he'd sit in the corner on his own. Made me suspicious.'

'He try anything?'

'Tried to escape.'

'How far did he get?'

'Well –'

'How far?'

'He got out of the cage.'

'He got *out*?'

'Uh-huh.'

'That's why you left your last job?'

'Oh no. We caught him. Put him back in a cage – one of those new numbers with electrified bars. You could electrify the floor as well – made the little bastards do a dance.'

'The point is – how did he escape in the first place?'

'Little bastard tricked me.'

'Just how did he do that?'

'Well now . . .'

'This I should hear. Those cages are supposed to be super-secure.'

'There's no problem with the cages.'

'It's highly unusual for a dwarf to escape. I notice you didn't put that on your application.'

'Let me tell you how it happened. I'd just started on the night-shift. I went in there, started jabbing the little bastards with my trident. They were all bang at it. If they're not fighting, they're fucking, or throwing shit at each other. And that's all we need, dwarves fucking, meaning more dwarves.'

'Go on.'

'So I was goading these little fucks with my cat-o'-nine-tails.'

'The trident.'

'Huh?'

'You said you used the three-pronged trident.'

'Oh yeah – well, the trident . . . I do keep a cat-o'-nine-tails also. Have it on my belt there. It's good if you want to get a whole bunch of them back from the bars in one go.'

'I am aware of the technique.'

'You do a bit yourself?'

'It's my position you'll be filling.'

'So I've got the job?'

'This is just an interview. You're on the shortlist, no pun intended. Now if you'll just tell me how the dwarf escaped.'

'Oh yes. Well here's what happened. The little fella was crouched in the corner, all on his own – I guessed he must be asleep – while the rest of them, well the rest of them were raising merry hell. They go crazy stuck in that cage the whole day on top of one another. I seriously think most of them are insane. We couldn't let them out now if we wanted to. I mean, how would people like that readjust?'

'How indeed.'

'So this little dwarf is all on his own in the corner of the cage. I go over to him, and give him a prod with the trident, just to wake him up. Turns out – not only is he awake – who could sleep through that racket after all? – that's another thing – when do these things sleep?'

'Sounds like they don't get a chance.'

'I mean how can they? That must send you crazy too. Sleep deprivation. Hell, doing the night-shift is bad enough. That's a form of torture.'

'The dwarf . . .'

'Oh yes. The dwarf. Well, he leaped out of the way of the trident prong as I made a lunge for him. Just got clean out of the way. "Why did you do that?" he asked me. Now this took me aback a little. I'm used to these little freaks spitting and screaming and throwing their own shit and so forth. So to have one talk to you like that is a bit of a shock. "I'm not doing any harm. I wasn't making any noise," he said. I just wasn't used to having them answering back to me. So I jabbed him once again, and once again he jumped out of the way, into the centre of the cage. "You little bastard," I told him. "I'll turn the hose on you!" Now all the others, who'd quietened down for a moment, started to get over-excited again, leaping around and screaming like a bunch of animals, and this one dwarf sits in among all this, staring out at me, saying nothing. This really got me furious. I very nearly went and got the hose there and then. In all honesty I wanted to wrap it round his fucking neck.'

'What did you do?'

'Jesus – I was ready to climb in that cage and take him apart. Well, I just let them wear themselves out, you know? Gave me a moment to calm myself down. Now, a little later on, the dwarf, the one that has been causing all the trouble . . .'

'Trouble?'

'The one that has me suspicious. And I had every reason to be suspicious. He comes up to the edge of the cage once more. I can see he's wanting to say something. So I say to him, "What is the problem you half-formed fuck?" So he wrinkles up his face and says, "Without your trident, your whip, your cage – without those things, you're nothing." "What are you getting at, Napoleon?" I said to him. "I may be small," he said, "but I could take you." "SMALL!" I shouted at him. "You're a fucking midget. You wouldn't get on a funfair ride." "Nevertheless, I could take you," he persisted. "You talk like a man," I told him, "but you're not one. Maybe you haven't looked in the mirror recently. If you could reach to see your reflection." "I will beat you," he said. I ignored him. I wasn't going to let the midget get the better of me. But he kept on at me in this vein, until some of the other midgets joined in. "He'll beat ya!" they called out, and started throwing shit around. I gave the dirty bastards a jab with the trident. I tried to get him, but each time he jumped out of the way just in time. I mean, it was plainly ridiculous. I'm two and a half times his size. Feel that. Pure muscle.'

'I'll take your word for it.'

'Well, I couldn't let this carry on. The little bastard's insubordination was bound to cause problems among the group as a whole. I could not have a cage full of dwarves thinking that one of them might be able to beat me up. What kind of guard would that make me? So, I decided to prove it to them, there and then – finish him off right in front of them. That might shut him up. I know it's highly irregular – to pursue such a course of action . . . but I think if you are in a position of responsibility it is necessary to do whatever is required, even if it is not in the manual.'

'I'm not sure I entirely agree. But proceed.'

'So I go up to the bars and I say to the little punk, "I'll fight you. I'll smash you into the ground." "Without your trident, without your whip?" he asked. "No problem," I told him. I took off my belt and cat-o'-nine-tails, and then

the trident, and my cap, and laid them down on the floor.
Then I took off my shirt, folded that up and put it on the
floor. Didn't want to get it torn or spattered with blood
or anything. Then I said to him, "Now I'm going to let you
out of the cage and we'll fight. And the rest of you
bastards get back from the gate." Of course they obeyed.
Sure they did. They wanted to see this. Man versus
Dwarf. Who wouldn't? As soon as they were all back, I
signalled my dwarf opponent to step forward to the gate,
and unlocked it and pulled him out. "I'm going to stand
over here and when —" Just then he got out of my grasp
and ran over to where my weapons were on the floor.
"Get away from there!" I told him. But quick as a flash he
pulled on the belt with the cat-o'-nine-tails attached,
grabbed the shirt and hat and trident and ran round the
other side of the cage. Of course, all the other dwarves in
the cage went crazy. In no time at all he had the shirt and
hat on, and was dancing round the cage, prodding the
dwarves with the trident, making fun of me! The other
dwarves thought this was the funniest thing they'd ever
seen. They were sticking their arses through the bars and
waggling them for him to prod. "Get back in there you
filthy half-humans," he shouted at them and they roared
with laughter. I tried to catch him but I couldn't get close.
I'd run round the cage and he'd run round the other side.
He'd take my cap off his head and wave it at me. Soon I
got worn out, and leaned up against the bars to catch my

breath. All of a sudden the whole cageful is there, and they grab me and hold me against the bars. I couldn't move. The little bastard comes and stands in front of me with the trident. There's an evil glint in his dwarf eyes now; something's going on. He pulls back the trident and I swear to God he was about to put it through my guts. I cried out and, as I cried out, two guards came rushing in – they'd heard the commotion – and they grabbed the dwarf and beat him to within an inch of his life . . .'

'No pun intended.'

'I got back my trident and cat-o'-nine-tails and went to work on the dwarves in the cage. Soon we had them back under control. Let me tell you, we didn't have much trouble from our troublemaker after that. Didn't have much choice. His jaw was smashed. Both his legs broken.'

'Very impressive, I'm sure.'

'Look, I know the little bastard got the better of me, but the point is it didn't get any further than that.'

'But nevertheless, it got that far.'

'Will this count against me? You know, I didn't need to mention this at all. The only reason I did is because I thought you would appreciate how we dealt with the situation that arose.'

'Mmm. I understand.'

'Do I get the job or don't I?'

'There's one more thing we need you to do this afternoon. A written test. I'll get my assistant Marlene to guide you through it – it's quite simple really. Marlene, would you come in here a second?'

'When d'you think you'll be able to let me know if I got the – whoaah – shit!'

'This is Marlene.'

'Holy shit – a –'

'Midget?'

'What the hell!'

'You didn't see her on the way in?'

'She was sat behind a desk, for goodness' sake. Good God, how could you?'

'It's called integration, Mr Gants.'

'It's "sick in the head" is what it's called.'

'It's the new way forward, Mr Gants.'

'Get the fuck away from me. What kind of place is this?'

'The written test, Mr Gants?'

'Fuck the written test! I'm gone – *history*!'

'I apologise for that, Marlene. It looks like Mr Gants won't be taking the written test after all.'

'That's quite all right, Mr Jenkins.'

'Marlene – how many more have I got to see today?'

'Four more. The next one, Mr Bruno, is a dwarf himself.'

'A dwarf dwarf-wrangler – this I have to see.'

'I'll send him through.'

'Thank you, Marlene. And hold my calls. Mr Bruno.

Pleased to meet you. Do sit down. Ah, you are sitting down. About your application . . .'

'What about it?'

'Well, you don't seem to have much experience in the field.'

'That's true I suppose. But I don't see that as a problem. How much can there be to walking round a cage all day, keeping an eye on things?'

'Well, actually the job involves more than that.'

'Sure, sure, I understand, but I can pick all that up, right?'

'What made you apply for this job in particular?'

'Are you saying I'm not suitable for the job?'

'Oh no –'

'It's just that you seem to be implying that I'm not qualified. If I remember correctly the advertisement said "Full training and uniform will be supplied". Now, the question *I* have to ask is, why did you drag me in here for an interview, if you don't think I'm suitable for the job?'

'I'm sure –'

'Because in point of fact I feel I am completely suited to the job . . .'

'Because you're one of them?'

'I beg your pardon?'

'Because you understand what makes them tick.'

'Makes who tick?'

'The dwarves.'

'You're suggesting –'

'Because you're a dwarf, you'll understand the other dwarves.'

'What – the *fuck* – me, a dwarf! I'm little, certainly, but a dwarf?'

'You're not seriously . . .'

'I've had this shit before. I don't intend to have it again. You know how much taller I am than the average dwarf? That much. And you know how much shorter I am than the average "small person"? This much. Does that make me a dwarf? I think not.'

'Well, let's move on.'

'Let's not move on. You think I'm a dwarf.'

'Well, yes.'

'I'm not a dwarf.'

'Mr Bruno, there's no need for us to argue, we're both grown men.'

'Ha! Was that a crack? Oh, yes, feel free to insult me.'

'I wasn't insulting you. I've got nothing against dwarves *per se*. I'm all for integration. As you'll have noticed from my assistant, Marlene.'

'Oh yeah. The little dwarf chick out in the lobby – how come she's loose? Shouldn't she be in a cage?'

'With all due respect, Mr Bruno, some people might say the same about you.'

'Again with the cracks. Listen – I got a normal-sized

hand that I'll make into a normal-sized fist and put in your big mouth.'

'There is no need to become violent, Mr Bruno.'

'Well, there's no need to be abusive.'

'Mr Bruno, what are your motives for wanting this job?'

'I need a job. A man's got to eat.'

'It strikes me as odd that you'd want a job that quite often involves chastising, so to speak, your fellow man.'

'My fellow man? For the final time, I'm just a small person — I have fun like any other human being. I got a girlfriend. And not some half-formed skank like your secretary.'

'My assistant —'

'Whatever. My girl, well, you should see her. Stacked. Beautiful. Forget about it. When I go down on her — don't say it . . .'

'Say what?'

'I heard it a thousand and one times. Don't you mean "When I go UP on her"? I need to hear that joke again like I need a hole in the head. The point I was making — well, let me put it to you this way — I wear regular-sized underpants.'

'That's very interesting.'

'In point of fact, you could say I'm "outsize" in that department.'

'I don't doubt it.'

'You don't believe me. I'll whip it out. How'd'you like that? I'm entirely sure it's why my girlfriend stays with me as long as she does. I'll get her to write me a reference. Here – look.'

'Please don't.'

'I'm not ashamed.'

'Please zip up.'

'Huh? What do you say? Do I get the job?'

'Marlene – send in the guards.'

'Look at that – beautiful.'

'For God's sake.'

'Jesus – what goes on?'

'Here – touch it.'

'Guards – get him out of my office.'

'Did this one escape?'

'Hey, get your hands off me.'

'Shall we put him in a cage?'

'For the time being.'

'NO! What? What the hell happened to integration?'

'Get him out of here.'

'You're coming with us, you little freak.'

'I'm not a dwarf! I'm an *interviewee*.'

'Marlene . . . send in the next one. Do come in. Sorry about all that. Please, take a seat.'

'I think I'm somewhat overdressed for the occasion.'

'Not at all.'

'It's just that if we're going to have to give a practical demonstration, I'd rather not get my suit messed up.'

'There's no practical demonstration involved.'

'But those men, wrangling the dwarf out of here just now.'

'Oh no. You see *he* came for the job interview. It's just he got a little overexcited.'

'The dwarf – oh, I see. Then there's been a dreadful mistake. Sorry. I should leave now. I won't waste any more of your time.'

'What seems to be the problem?'

'When I read the advertisement for a dwarf-wrangler, I assumed you wanted someone to wrangle dwarves. Not a wrangler who *was* a dwarf. I should have realised when I saw your midget receptionist. My mistake.'

'There's no mistake. The last candidate was a dwarf. That's all.'

'So *he* misread the advertisement.'

'Not exactly. We welcome all comers here –'

'Equal opportunities? I thought that got banned. Since they found that factory full of ni—'

'Please. Sit down.'

'If you're sure it's okay.'

'Really. It's fine. Now, your experience seems to be primarily in accounting. What makes you want to switch to this?'

'The money systems are in flux at the moment. I

predict a total collapse within months. This, on the other hand, is a growth market.'

'I hope that's true.'

'Oh, it's going to happen. You can put anything in those cages, you know what I mean? Not just dwarves. People, whatever.'

'You're certainly enthusiastic. Do you think you could adapt well to this line of work?'

'Absolutely.'

'It involves long hours and there is a physical aspect to the work.'

'Physical — ?'

'You'll come into contact with the dwarves now and again. You might have to get them back from the bars, for example.'

'Now that I *have* had experience in.'

'How so?'

'I put my wife in a cage.'

'Your wife?'

'She was getting very fat and violent. I did it for her own good. Locked her in a cage in the house.'

'How long did you keep her in there?'

'Oh no, she's in there the whole time. I have to feed her through the bars. Show me a person who ever came out of a cage fat. I bet those dwarves are in shape.'

'I'll bet they are . . .'

'So d'you get anything to beat the dwarves with?'

'Beat them?'

'I use a long stick on my wife. Sometimes I get inside the cage and use a short length of pipe on her. That's if she really gets out of hand. Look, I brought it along. I bash her like this . . .'

'I don't think that was really necessary.'

'I'm sorry. I think I broke your phone. Have you got any of those caged dwarves around here? Let me show you what I can do. I'm all fired up. I can't beat the wife any more. Her whole body is covered with welts. I'd love to get my hands on some of those little bastards though.'

'I don't think you're exactly what we're looking for.'

'No? Look at this motion. Zz-aap! Ahh shit, I smashed a picture. Never mind. Fuck the furniture, let me wreck a midget –'

'I think perhaps you'd better leave after all.'

'Wha-aat! Are you joking? I'll take this fucking pipe to *your* head. I'll bash your brains in. Then you'll HAVE to give me the job. ARRRGGH! What the hell is that? You tore my fucking jacket!'

'Cat-o'-nine-tails. We use it on the dwarves sometimes.'

'AAARRGGGHHHH!'

'Hurts, doesn't it?'

'AARGHH!'

'And this. . . this is the three-pronged trident.'

'Jesus! No! Arghh! No – AIEEEE!'

'Maybe we should put you in the cage.'

'Mercy, mercy, AAAARGH!'

'Get back!'

'Pur-lease –'

'MARLENE.'

'Yes, Mr Jenkins.'

'Show this gentlemen out.'

'You'll pay – I'll k— . . . ARRRRRGGGHHH! My eye . . . can't suh, suh, see . . .'

'. . . and Marlene . . .'

'Yes, Mr Jenkins?'

'Cancel the rest of today's appointments.'

'Yes, Mr Jenkins.'

'I'm going home.'

the cruise

Thursday

We set off today. The weather was bloody awful. John felt sick almost immediately. I told him to go and lie down in the cabin. Our request for a cabin with a sea-view on the top deck was turned down. I told them John gets agoraphobic.

Lunch was bloody awful. I felt sick afterwards. I think it was the vegetables with the lasagne. I'm sure they were recooked. You'd have thought with the price we paid that they wouldn't have recooked veg. I complained to the rep onboard and he said we'd get a seat at the captain's table some time during the week.

I met a couple from Derby this afternoon in the gift shop and we arranged to go for drinks. John was violently sick this evening so he went to lie down again and I went for drinks with them on my own.

Friday

I went to see the ship's doctor this morning. When I woke up I had an awful pain down my side and I remembered I'd been thrown against the piano in the cocktail bar. The doctor said I'd bruised my ribs and told me to take it easy for a while and he had to fill out a form. I told him the ship had lurched and I was thrown against the piano. I asked him if I might be elegible for compensation and he said he wasn't the person to ask about that, he was just a doctor.

Apart from that it was quite good last night. We had a few drinks at Happy Hour and then they had cabaret, but the singer wasn't very good, I thought I could do better than that, even though John says it sounds like next door are torturing the cat when I'm singing in the bath and he's half a mind to call the RSPCA. You would have thought that for £1,500 per person they could afford to hire a decent singer even if it was a professional or someone off the television. Although I did find out that some of the couples on the cruise had booked last minute and off Teletext and got £399 off, which I thought was a bit unfair. We booked way ahead and even then we didn't get a cabin with a sea-view even though I put on the forms 'Husband agoraphobic'. I'm definitely thinking of writing to the holiday company about that when we get back, or at least Anne Robinson – maybe they'd be interested in doing a film on it.

John's still sick in bed but I bought him a book to read. He should be OK but he reckons the fumes from the boiler room are getting into the cabin through the air vents and making it worse. I've asked if we can change cabins, preferably to one on the top and maybe the people who booked late can have our cabin, I don't see why not.

Saturday

We sat at the Captain's table today, me and John – he's feeling a bit better and besides he didn't want to miss sitting at the Captain's table. I thought it would be just us and the Captain but there was about twenty of us in all. I said, 'If you're sitting here with us, who's driving the ship?' John said, 'He doesn't look like the bloke out of the advert,' and I said which advert? and he goes, 'Birds Eye Fish Fingers!' The food was OK but John had to ruin it by rushing off to the loo to be sick during the main course. I saw him later on in the cabin and he was bright green and he said he thought maybe it was salmonella.

I met the couple from Derby on the sundeck and I said that we should go for some cocktails later on, but they didn't seem too keen, probably because they saw us at the Captain's table and felt left out.

There was supposed to be whale-watching later on this afternoon but no-one could see any so I told John he hadn't missed much.

Monday

It's been raining for the last few days. I just can't believe it. It's been miserable and we've mostly been stuck in our cabin because it's been so wet outside, which was OK but John had blocked up the toilet and the stink was awful, especially as we are right over the boiler room and it hots right up. I could hardly breathe and they didn't exactly hurry to send someone to fix it, but they said the reason was a lot of the toilets had got blocked up because the plumbing on our level had got backed up. It hasn't been much of a holiday at all. Hopefully the weather will clear up soon and things will get back to normal.

Tuesday

It's still raining. They laid on a special buffet for us at lunchtime, Caribbean cuisine, but it all got soaked through. They had on some Caribbean music as well which was bloody awful. I saw the couple from Derby and they avoided me and looked ever so sheepish and I think it's probably because they were one of the couples who got a cheap deal and know I knew because I complained to the rep about it.

Thursday

Well, the holiday's been a total disaster, a total waste of money. I asked the rep if there was any way we could get a refund and he said you could only claim due to illness or injury and I said that John had been sick most of the journey and he said the company wasn't liable for seasickness and I told him it was because of the recooked vegetables that he had got ill and he said no-one else had complained and three hundred people had eaten them so it was probably seasickness and that perhaps we shouldn't have booked a holiday on a ship if my husband got seasick and I told him we'd saved up years to come on this trip and it's like a second honeymoon. He just said, 'There's nothing I can do.' I said what about when I fell against the piano in the cocktail lounge – the doctor had said I'd bruised my ribs because of that and it was because the ship had lurched that it happened so the company was liable and he said that witnesses had confirmed that I was drunk and had walked into that piano and that the ship hadn't lurched at all, and I said, 'What witnesses?' and he said the Moulds, the couple from Derby. I couldn't believe it. I'd gone out with them, not because I wanted to but because John was ill. I went up to their cabin there and then and knocked on the door and she was there with a face pack on and he was putting a bow tie on and I said, 'Where are you going?' and they said, 'The Captain's Banquet,' and I said, 'I didn't hear about the Captain's Banquet,' and they said, 'You have to sign up for it when you book,' and I said, 'The travel agent never told me about that,' and she just shrugged her shoulders and then I said, 'Why are you going around telling people I was drunk?' and she said it wasn't their fault, the rep had made them fill out an incident form and asked how long we'd been drinking and she said all evening, and I said, 'You silly cow, you could have lied, it wasn't my fault I fell against the piano,' and she said, 'You were making a fool of yourself!' and I said, 'I don't have to stand here listening to this!' and the husband said, 'Good, piss off then!'

Well, it's ruined my holiday and all she needed to do was lie.

Friday

'the cruise'

Saturday

Everyone's been terribly kind to me and the rep's been nice and they said what a terrible thing it was to happen.

John said that he was feeling a bit better and could we go down to the main deck and at least try and enjoy the last bit of the holiday and that he felt like something to eat, maybe just a sandwich, so we were just going down the steps and it was still a bit wet but the weather was clearing up a bit although it was still overcast and John was a bit unsteady on his feet and he slipped on the step and it looked like he was going to fall so I tried to grab him but he just fell forward and went down the whole length of the stairs. I went down as quickly as I could and when I got to him his head was at a funny angle against the floor and someone else came and then the doctor but John had broken his neck and was dead.

Sunday

I've been asked to fill out some forms and so forth and say what happened. The ship's rep said they'll take some statements off other passengers and I told them someone had come along and helped when it happened and they should speak to her.

Monday

Bad news. The couple from Derby said that they saw everything and that they were coming out of their cabin and they saw me push John down the stairs and now the rep and everyone are treating this as a very serious matter indeed and they are turning the ship back early and they are going to call the police when we get back into port. It's so ridiculous, do they really think I'd push my husband down the stairs, we've been married twenty years and this is our second honeymoon and we saved up for ages to afford the cruise and we didn't get it off Teletext either. Can't they see I'm upset and they have to go and say a thing like that.

I mean I must admit I was sort of hoping John would slip on those steps because then we could claim some money back – at least part of what we'd spent, but I didn't want him to fall like *that*, just slip and twist his ankle or something so we'd get a bit of money, but not break his neck. He hadn't really wanted to leave the cabin but I persuaded him and said fresh air might help, what with all the boiler fumes and whatnot, and when he started to slip I just gave him a little push to help him on his way but I didn't think he'd fall like that, the great dodo.

Even if I did do it they didn't need to say anything, if they'd just minded their own business, it's ruined everything, and just as it started to get a bit sunny as well.

42

house of buggin'

He couldn't sleep now, he knew that much. There wasn't even any point in trying in this heat, and the AC didn't work – the day the landlord fixed it, that would be the day hell freezes over.

He lay on his back and stared at the ceiling. He could hear noise from the street below. Bottles breaking, people whooping. Didn't they have jobs to do in the morning, didn't they have rent to pay like him? How did they afford to party all the time?

Now he'd lie there and think about what a dump it was that he lived in, and how the hell he was going to be able to pay for something better. He could hardly pay for this. Don't start thinking negative, he thought, you start thinking one negative thought, all of a sudden you got a hundred negative thoughts in your head. He could be worse off. Some country on the news, they got hit by a typhoon, typhoid or something. Now they had nothing, no homes, no nothing, people waving to the helicopters from the trees. He'd seen it all right there on the news.

It didn't even make him feel any better. He'd worked a double shift and he felt like shit. Broke his balls to live in the shit.

The neighbours were a bunch of bums. No manners. Just that evening, he'd seen a woman pissing in the street. She was just standing there, piss running down her legs. She hadn't even pulled her pants down. He thought he was going to puke on the spot seeing the piss spraying everywhere like a broken fire hydrant, that big pool of piss on the pavement, splashing round her ankles. With neighbours like that, who needs enemies? Sweet Jesus, they should pay *him* to live there, he should send a bill to the landlord at the end of each month.

And the place was infested with roaches. You could never catch 'em, but you could hear them. They were all over the place. It was illegal to let them grow that big. He'd read about it. Anything over a foot was illegal.

La Super Cucaracha.

The landlord would say, 'You got roaches, well, you should think about not leavin' food lyin' aroun', you people is savages, leavin' pizza lyin' roun' on the floor, what do you expec'? I seen it, that ain' my problem.' He said, 'We don't eat pizza,' and the landlord says, 'I ain't got time to lissen to tha', always complainin', I shud throw you all out on tha' street.'

Christ – now he'd lie in bed and think about shit – and have to go to work on no sleep. What a shitty predicament. He rolled on to his side. She was all curled up on the other side of the bed.

The plumbing from the flat above came to life. Somebody groaned and rattled a chain. All that nice stuff mixed together, flushed through the pipes, across the ceiling and turned at a right angle down behind the wall by his head and then through the floor and away.

She didn't even stir, not a murmur. Whatever it was, she slept. Noise, heat, typhoon.

He waited for the sound of the pipes to die away. He closed his eyes and curled into a ball. Maybe that was the trick.

Then he remembered, *she'd* kept him awake the night before. She'd called out a name in her sleep – 'Ricky' – then she'd moaned out loud. Who the hell was Ricky? It had got him horribly excited in the middle of the night, so that he wanted to wake her up and say, 'Who the hell is Ricky?' They'd spent so little time together recently, him working double shifts and coming in late and getting up early, would it be any wonder if she . . . He couldn't stand that, he couldn't stand it if she was going with another man. That was the worst thing on earth, the worst feeling on earth, to find out your woman is with another man, that feeling in the guts that's like they've twisted themselves into knots.

The next day he hadn't asked her anything, but he'd wanted to. It could be anyone, he didn't want to make a fool of himself, but he didn't want to drive himself crazy, he just wanted to say, 'Who the hell is Ricky? Is it someone from your cleaning job? Who is it? Tell me it's a cousin you never mentioned, or someone off the TV, please tell me that . . .' But he didn't, he sat there letting his eggs go cold, and just drank some of his coffee, so maybe she knew he thought something was wrong. And he went to work and all through the day whenever he thought about it he stopped dead whatever he was doing and thought, what if she called that name out again that night? And the way she'd moaned like they were . . .

The bed shuddered. He opened his eyes. She must have been dreaming. Kicked her legs or something.

But dreaming about what? Why was she kicking her legs like that? She only did that when they went to the movies and some scary stuff occurred. That or when they were . . . was she with Ricky? Ricky making love to his wife in a dream. Oh no, no, he moaned. It's nothing, nothing at all. He was in love with her, she was in love with him. She told him so. He had to take some deep breaths. Someone shouted outside and a baby started wailing. He thought he would go crazy.

He closed his eyes again and took a deep breath and

held it. He was very conscious of the heat, of being curled up on the sweaty sheets with his eyes shut.

What the hell!

He couldn't get comfortable. If you can't get comfortable in your own bed, because your wife is making it with another man in her dreams. Jesus.

He had to get them out of there. He had to get something better for them both, like he'd promised. She hated the place as much as he did, more! No wonder she was dreaming things like that. Dreaming, hoping, remembering, what?

He went over the options again. Night after night he tried to think of a way out. He went round in circles and always ended up at the same place. Shit city.

The other day he had cornered his manager, a German named Glubohns.

'What are my prospects here?' he'd asked him.

'Prospects?' the German replied. 'What is this prospects?'

'Where can I expect this job to lead? I got a wife, a family.'

'You have a child?'

'I want a family. What are my chances of moving up?' he said.

'Promotions? Here? Ha!'

'I need to move out of my apartment. The noise, the neighbours.'

'You don't like the neighbours, buy a mansion house.' The manager had walked off, and that had been that.

He hated his boss's dismissive manner, and the terrible impulses his boss caused to rise in him. Someday, maybe, he would –

The bed shuddered again. He had been looking at his wife when it happened. She hadn't moved. He felt the bed tilting. Like something out of *The Exorcist,* he thought, and grabbed the crucifix around his neck and crossed himself. 'Mamma,' he said, and prodded her gently, afraid to move. She'd start floating above the bed!

She didn't move. She hadn't moved.

Why the hell had the bed moved like that? Maybe the floor was collapsing underneath them.

His first impulse was to look under the bed, to see where they had gone through the floor. But he didn't dare move. It was like a car balanced on the edge of a cliff, like in that movie. If he moved, that would be it.

He lay still. If it was not one thing, it was the other. Was it not bad enough that his wife was cheating on him, that he had to work the double shift, that he could not get a night's sleep, that his bed was going through the fucking floor. Was this not enough? Tears formed at the outer edges of his eyes, gathered, and rolled down towards his ears.

The was a scream downstairs.

The bed moved again.

'Hey, wake up,' he said. She rolled over, drowsy, looking at him through one opened eye.

'Wha—'

'Gently,' he said. 'The house is falling down.'

'The house is what?'

'Falling down. Get off the bed. Careful.'

She shrugged and moved off the bed, and stood there swaying, still woozy from sleep. He got up and stood by the bed and grinned. They'd sue the landlord's ass for this. Big time! Goddamn place falling apart round their ears. The floor was going through, that was dangerous. He'd read about it. Balconies falling off with whole families on them having a barbecue, roofs falling down and stuff like that.

He felt something brush against his bare ankle from under the bed, and cried out.

'What is it?'

He leaped back against the wall. Something was under the bed. Or someone. Someone . . . ?

Someone *hiding* under the bed.

He looked over at her.

That wouldn't be right. She wouldn't do that, it wasn't right. But maybe while he was out, and she knew he'd be out late because he was working a double shift, and he'd come back and she'd been heavy breathing, and maybe they'd forgotten what time it was and they'd heard the door and there was nothing they could do and she pretended to be asleep, and he'd crawled under the bed, and all the time . . .

Ricky!

Ricky under the bed, waiting for him to fall asleep, then sneaking out, crawling across the floor. Imposter!

'Who is it?' he groaned.

She stared back at him, but all he could see were the whites of her eyes, filled with terror, with guilt. He felt a sob rising in his chest.

He motioned her to move away from the bed. He reached and flipped the mattress off the bed frame. Beneath the bedsprings, on the floor, in the dark, something crouched there.

'You motherfucker! You didn't think . . .'

It was shiny, still. About two feet long. God save him – his wife, making it with Ricky the midget! Cowering under there. Ricky the midget coward, the sweating midget coward.

'The lights –'

She didn't move.

'THE LIGHTS! Let's get a look at him.'

She felt her way along the wall until she got to the switch.

She turned it on.

'Jesus Christ,' he said, crossing himself. She screamed.

The thing started towards him.

A metre and a half long. A hard shiny shell, twitching antennae as thick as coat-hangers.

'Jesus Christ,' he said again. He kicked at the thing, and grabbed his wife's arm, and pulled her with him out of the room. They had to get out. No matter that he was only wearing his shorts and she was wearing a nightie. He opened the front door on to the second-floor hallway. The carpet moved with shiny black shells and bristling limbs. One of them flew through the doorway before he could slam the door shut again. He took the hall table and sat it down on the thing hard, one of the wooden table legs going through it.

They went into the front room. They could hear that big one battering the door to the bedroom, scraping the wood with its wiry antennae.

'The window,' he said. He opened the window and looked down into the alleyway that ran the length of the side of the building. There was a big trash container right there under the window, the lid was open. God thank the tramp who'd been rifling through the trash. They could leap into it. Like in the cop show. He couldn't see into the container, it was dark. But it'd be full of cardboard and paper and soft stuff to land on. They were only one floor up. In the cop show he did it from five.

His wife looked at him, pleading for another way out.

He shrugged, then opened the windows as wide as they would go and helped her up on the ledge. Then he climbed up with her.

They leaped together, holding hands. Let us land safe, he prayed, the other hand clutching his crucifix.

They crash-landed into the darkness, and lay there holding each other, both aware that the crisp, cracking noise on impact wasn't paper, or garbage, or soft stuff to land on, and nor was the scuttling and clicking noise as the things clambered over one another onto them.

His wife laughed hysterically and said, 'It tickles.'

pigback apocalypse

We'd been three days out of the Schlemm canal. Some of the Gurks were bitching about their packs, and all I could do was tell them to can it. For all we knew there were snouts all over. They'd wiped out half the unit in the canal already and morale was seriously low.

Two of the Gurks had tried to leave under the guise of a recon mission and I'd had to shoot them. That was no big deal. That kind of mutinous behaviour was the last thing anybody needed, and we were all as good as gone anyway. Why give the snouts the satisfaction?

We camped down for the night by the bluff about sixteen miles south of the canal. We set up tents and a fire, and one of the Gurks brought out a guitar and started to play, so I shot him. Last thing we needed was snouts getting wind of a Gurk singalong. That would be the end of us, if nothing else, as if we weren't finished anyway. The guitar was firewood. I also caught a couple of Gurks drinking from ale-cans. I half-decided to have them CM'd, but decided instead that the safer option was to shoot them. I will do, and have done, everything I can to keep this unit together. Note to canteen corps: synth-peas from hotcan undercooked.

The snouts moved in on the camp during the night. They must have seen our yellow flag. I didn't sleep, I was cooking some feamo-stew over the fire – the auto-heaters never get the gravy hot enough, and the gravy has to be *hot*, so I don't bother using them any more – and I heard the snouts truffling around in the undergrowth to the east of the camp.

I wasn't prepared to take the risk. I went from tent to tent, rousing the Gurks. One of the Gurks refused to wake, and instead shouted out, 'ROLL ME OVER,' so I snuffed him out with a pillow before he gave our position away.

We packed up and moved out, but not before launching an anti-personnel rocket into the undergrowth, making snout-pork.

It's hungry work walking. As a precaution I put the Gurks on half-rations, to make sure we don't run out of supplies. One of the Gurks asked if that meant I was on half-rations too, but I didn't dignify that with an answer: it just means more food for the rest of us.

We'd been on the move for three more days. Morale was still seriously low, and there was not much I could do about that. I told the men, I told them, the snouts are everywhere, all we can do is be on our guard, all the time, that's it. One of the Gurks started to question the nature of the war, putting a big question mark after the whole concept of the word 'war', asking WHY, WHY, *WHY*? I shot him.

Finally, it seems, we are out of snout territory. The men had to carry me the last half-day; I needed to conserve my energy.

I said to the men, we can camp tonight, and we can relax, and, more importantly, eat – a decent cook-up, beefsteak, mashed potatoes, gravy, and the small blueberry cheesecakes for dessert – but you must still be on your guard.

I went to scout the surrounding area, just to be sure, and everything seemed fine. Sometimes you can just *feel*. That's what it is to be a soldier, that's what it is to be a leader. Call it instinct, call it sixth sense, it's not something that can be bought, it just comes, and you don't know you've got it until it's on you. Then it was time to eat.

*

The food was good but the beefsteak was a little tough. I had two of the cheesecakes as a reward to myself. I thought I heard one of the Gurks say something like, 'Corporal Lard-arsey sure got guts don't he,' and they all laughed. I couldn't be sure, but I was sure enough. The war was over for him, at the end of my bayonet, driven deep into *his* guts.

After dinner I went to secure the area.

God forbid this war ends, but if it does, they will probably try and give me a medal. That wasn't why I chose to be a soldier and lead a unit, to get a medal. A medal doesn't mean anything, it just says you did your job, and you did it well, and I know that already. As long as I've got boots on my feet and a decent mess hall, then I'm happy.

When I got back to the camp, the men were in a boisterous mood. One was pretending to be a snout, down on all fours, and the other men were prodding him with a stick.

I had no choice.

The gunfire was a mistake, but we all make mistakes. I heard them soon, coming through the undergrowth, homing in. Soon they would be upon me.

It didn't matter though. I had bullets left. No soldiers, but plenty of bullets.

a cruel occurrence at victoria coach station

Young Goran got off the bus at Victoria Coach Station, struggling with his rucksack.

He made his way across the concourse, towards the road, when a man stepped up to him and held out a card. The man, name of Eddie Constantine, wore a dark grey suit, and sported a thin black moustache, his hair combed in a parting.

'Bed and breakfast, ten pounds,' he said.

Goran took the card from the man and studied it. It read —

Bed and Breakfast £10
Excelsior Hotel

'Ten pounds?'

'It's just around the corner.'

Goran did the calculations in his head. Ten pounds was not only very reasonable, it was bloody cheap for London. It was a third less than the hostel he was planning to go to, and that didn't even include breakfast.

'Is near?'

'Like I said. Just around the corner.'

Goran was tired. He'd been on the coach for eighteen hours from Amsterdam. He hadn't been able to sleep. All he wanted to do was find a place to stay, stow the rucksack, shower, and rest.

'What are the facilities?' he asked the man who had given him the card.

'Facilities. It'd be easier to tell you what we haven't got. There's a pool, indoor, heated, Olympic-sized, diving boards and that. Sauna – mixed, mind. Games room, pool table, two squash courts – you play?'

'No. I mean what facilities in the room?'

'In the room – well, you've got your en-suite bath-room, towels and that, double bed –'

'Is the duvet duck?'

'Eh?'

'Feather. Is it feather?'

'Oh yes, lovely, you won't have a night's sleep like it. Big pillows like that, sort of pillows, when your head touches the pillow, bosh! You're gone, dead to the world. Earthquakes wouldn't wake you after that. Mattress, dead springy.'

'I am allergic to feather.'

'Allergic.'

'I have to have polyester.'

'That is not a problem. We have those. What else you got in the room there? Cable and that, free movies all night if you want it, room service, mini-bar. Balcony in every room, got a view of the Thames there. There's even a phone next to the toilet so you can make a call while you're taking care of business, if you know what I mean?'

'Why is so cheap?'

'Well that's because . . . you know, we don't have to advertise. That's how it works. We get customers like you off the coaches there. Then you'll go back to –'

'Holland.'

'Back to Holland, and you'll tell people where you stayed and all that, and they'll tell other people. It's called word of mouth.'

'Word of mouth, yes.'

'That's how we keep overheads down. Most hotels go under because they have to advertise. And people think, if they have to advertise, the hotel must be a load of crap, otherwise it would be full up because of the word of mouth, right?'

'Yes. I think I will take a room. Maybe for two nights.'

'Let's go,' Eddie said, and led the way.

*

'What does the breakfast consist of?' Goran asked, trailing behind the man, still struggling with his rucksack.

'That depends,' Eddie said, who was well into his stride along the pavement.

'On what?'

'Whether you want a continental or English breakfast.'

'What is the continental?'

'For that, you get your freshly squeezed orange juice, croissant, jam, coffee, fruit, yer banana and so forth.'

'And the English?'

'Well, that's your full English breakfast. You get two eggs, free-range mind, and that. Bacon, sausage, tomato, fried bread, bubble and squeak –'

'What is the bubble and squeak?'

'That's a sort of cabbage and potato flan. You get toast, cereal, OJ, yer juice there, tea and coffee, grapefruit, and a newspaper.'

'Black pudding?'

'Eh?'

'I hear of the black pudding.'

'Oh yeah, black pudding certainly. And we got all types of cereal. Frosties, Cornflakes, and whatnot.'

'And when is the breakfast?'

'About seven o'clock to eleven. They'll bring it up to your room if you want. Down here.'

They turned into a side street. 'It's just along here.'

'I also want to go on one of the open-top buses,' Goran said.

'Oh yeah, we do that, we can sort that. We do all sorts of excursions. Tower Bridge and all that.'

'We would like to see Rock Circus.'

'Piccadilly Circus, no problem. We do that. It's very close. Here we are, just here.'

Eddie unlocked the door and they went in.

The hallway was dark. Eddie switched on the light. There was a small table on one side with a stack of cards on it. They were the same as the card Eddie had given Goran.

'Many people stay?'

'Packed mate. Loads. Always busy. Here, let me take your rucksack. I'll show you to your room.'

'I pay now?'

'Pay when you leave.'

Goran lifted his rucksack off his back and gave it to Eddie. Eddie took it by the straps and immediately had to set it down on the floor. 'Christ, what have you got in there, the Crown jewels?'

Goran shrugged.

'Come on,' Eddie said, and went up the stairs. Goran followed.

They went along the landing to the door at the end. 'This is your room,' Eddie said, unlocking a padlock on the door. He took the padlock off, opened the door a couple of inches and gestured Goran to go in.

Goran moved past him along the hallway, and the man took a small length of pipe from his jacket pocket and cracked Goran over the back of the head with it. Goran swayed, and Eddie gave him a shove, sending him flying into the room.

'Get in there with the rest of 'em,' Eddie said, and slammed the door shut and put the padlock back on. 'Take care of our new guest will you, K?' he shouted out as he went down the stairs. He picked up another card, and headed back to the coach station. As he slammed the door shut, the rucksack fell on its side on the floor.

Eddie hung around the coach station for a couple of hours, and made a few approaches, but without any luck. I wonder if someone else is at this game, he thought, and poaching my customers.

When it started to get dark he decided to head home. I'll have a butcher's through the rucksack, he thought, and see what pickings.

He unlocked the door and clicked on the light in the hallway.

He hung up his jacket and went over to the rucksack and noticed the front of it had been cut open, a flap of fabric hanging down, and there was nothing in there.

'Wha the fuh?' he said out loud. 'K? K? You been at this?' he shouted up the stairwell.

He made a run up the stairs. The door to the room at the end of the corridor was ajar, and the padlock had been torn off. He panicked, and ran into the room. The one he'd brought in earlier was still there, face down, and the others were strapped to their beds. But the Keeper was slumped at the far end of the room, his throat cut, his bare chest slicked with blood, running all the way down to his studded belt and leather trousers. His tongue was hanging out.

This is no way to run a fucking hotel, Eddie thought. He felt a stinging pain in his foot, looked down and saw something flash from under the bed he was standing by. A red ribbon of blood shot out from his shoe.

'Christ! Shit!' He knelt, grabbed his ankle and lifted the edge of the blanket hanging down over the side of the bed. As he looked under there the blade came out again, into his eye, through it, and he fell back with the blade in his head, screaming, clutching at the knife.

The man who was a midget waited a while for the sound of Eddie's leather shoes kicking on the wooden floor to stop; then crawled out from under the bed.

He'd been in the process of trying to rouse Goran when Eddie had come in. He rolled his friend back over and slapped him a few times with a small hand.

'Goran, it is me.'

Goran had a nasty welt on the back of his head, but his friend, Kristoff, the midget, was sure he would be OK. He had better be, Kristoff thought, otherwise how will I survive in the city on my own?

He looked over at Eddie, sprawled on the floor, and thought, I must not forget my knife.

the orgy

At first Jon didn't want me coming along. When he mentioned it I said I'd definitely be interested, but he said, 'You have to bring your wife if you want to come,' and I said, 'I haven't got a wife,' and he said, 'Exactly.' But in the end he did invite me because he wanted to borrow my camcorder to film the event, and in any case I think he wanted to get the numbers up – probably thought no-one else would turn up anyway. When he said he was doing it, I just thought, oh yeah, it's another one of Jon's mad ideas, like the time he said he was going to build a wooden sauna in his back garden, or dig his own swimming pool which he never did. He did start digging a swimming pool but gave up and turned it into a duck pond. But it turned out he *was* going to go ahead with the orgy idea, and I thought, mad bastard! and I said, 'Do you think anyone will come?' and he says, ''Course they bloody will, everyone's at it these days,' and I said, 'How will they know about it?' and he said, 'I'll stick an ad in the *Argus*.' I said, 'Yeah? If you put it in bold, it costs a bit more per word, but it makes it stand out,' and he said, 'Don't be stupid, I'm not advertising it,' and I said, 'How then?' and he winks and goes, 'Word of mouth, word of mouth.' He said he'd looked into how things worked, the swingers' scene and all, because they do a lot of it in America and he'd read some articles on it, so he was all prepared. It was going to be round his house on a Friday night, he reckoned that was the day most people could make, and they'd push back all the furniture in the front room and they could use the bedroom as well; 'Bloody hell, they can use the kitchen if they so desire,' Jon said. 'I don't know whether it should be a masked orgy or not,' he said, 'maybe we'll see how it goes at this one.'

He told me I could come on one condition, and that was that I filmed everything, and I said, 'Can I join in?' and he said, 'OK, but keep your hands off the missus. And me for that matter!' He was going to have the nipper stay at his sister's for the night and I said, 'What, your sis isn't coming?' and he gave me such a look so I went, 'Joke, joke!'

I was pretty excited about the whole thing, I have to say, and at work they'd go, 'What are you smiling about?' And I'd go, 'Nothing,' because I wasn't going to tell anyone, was I? and they go, 'Get on with your work and stop fucking around.' I thought, I don't know if I *will* join in, I'll just see how it goes.

On the night of the orgy I got round there quite early and asked if I could plug in the camcorder to charge it up so the batteries didn't run out halfway through, like they did when Jon got me to film him practising his golf strokes so he could learn what he was doing wrong. He went apeshit when he found out, because I didn't tell him, I bottled it, I just carried on filming saying, 'Yeah, great,' and I didn't have a spare battery or anything, and when he found out, at the end when he says, 'Let's have a look then,' wanting to watch it back through the viewfinder, I had to tell him, and he said, 'You're fucking useless, you're worse than useless,' and tells his wife all about it when she comes to pick him up, he says, 'You'll never guess what this doughnut has gone and done,' and he went on and on about it, so one day I just said, 'Look, Jon, just give it a rest, yeah?' and he goes, 'Fucking prat,' so I don't want that to happen again.

Jon's wife was making some nibbles (and Jon says, 'No sausages on a stick, love, do you know what I mean? Ha ha') and Jon meanwhile was arranging the furniture in the front room to 'maximise the fuck-space', he said. 'Give us a hand with the sofa,' he said and we pushed it back and I said, 'Look there's a quid,' and Jon picked it up and put it in his pocket, going, 'I'm having that.'

Then he started putting boxes of rubber johnnies and

tubes of cream and whatnot out of a plastic bag all around the place for people to help themselves.

A bit later when the guests were about to arrive Jon made us all a drink, and he said he was a bit nervous, and so was I because he'd dimmed down the lights and I wasn't sure that the camera would pick up in a low-light situation, plus Jon went, 'Don't fuck it up like you did the golf,' and, 'Got some spare batteries this time?' but in a sarcastic way, and then the doorbell goes and Jon goes, 'Here we go,' and him and his missus both put on masks, hers was a sort of gold half-faced masked-ball-type mask, and Jon's was a Zorro one, and I said, 'You didn't tell me it was going to be masks, I haven't got one,' and Jon says, 'Don't worry, you'll be behind the camera most of the night so no-one will see you,' and goes off into the hallway and lets the people in going, 'Hello, hello, this way.' It pissed me off, it was like that time Jon arranged for a load of us to rent a villa in Spain and have a right good booze-up and we were all supposed to chip in, and then when I said to Jon, 'When do you want the money?' about a week later, he said, 'You what? We've already paid for it, we didn't think you wanted to go, there's no space left,' and I said, 'But I've booked me holiday off work,' and Jon just goes, 'Sorry, mate,' and then asks me to collect them all from the airport when they get back. I wouldn't have minded but all they went on about was that holiday all the time and what a laugh it was, for months afterwards, and they still go on about it now, especially about when Phil came back pissed and fell in the pool and they thought he had drowned.

By the time everyone arrived there were about a dozen people all together which was quite a good turn-out, all wearing masks, mostly those half-faced masks, but I didn't recognise anyone, well, I didn't want to catch anyone's eye because they'd certainly recognise me, although I think one might have been Tony, I couldn't be sure, it was quite dark, and I wasn't going to say, 'All right Tony?' Last time I did that in the pub he says, 'All right cunt?' in front of everyone. So I stood in the corner filming, and Jon started telling everyone what was going to happen. 'First of all,' he said, 'everyone is going to throw their keys into the middle of the room,' so every-one took out their keys and threw them in the middle of the room, and I threw mine in as well. 'I'm not sure why we do that,' Jon said, 'but that's what people always do at these things!' Everyone laughed and Jon said, 'Well, why don't we all strip off and get on with it,' and he started taking off his shirt, then his shoes and trousers, and they all joined in and no-one seemed to mind, because they all had masks on and had had a few drinks, and people were laughing and giggling and helping each other out of their clothes.

So I put the camera down and stripped off, and every-one chucked their clothes into the middle of the room so

I chucked mine in there too, then picked up the camera again and Jon just grabbed this woman and started kissing her and giving her a good feel-up and someone immediately went over and grabbed Jon's wife and laid her down on the sofa and started kissing her tits, and everyone was pairing off and someone said, 'Not me, stupid, someone else'; but I didn't know which way to point the camera, I couldn't film it all, so I filmed a bit of this, and a bit of that, and I still didn't recognise anyone, although the bloke kissing Jon's wife's tits I'm sure was Tony because he's always getting his arse out at the pub and then Jon's wife goes, 'Ooh, Tony,' when he starts sucking her tits so I *knew* it was him, but I suppose the rest were Jon's mates from work or something. I went into the kitchen to get some nibbles, but there was a couple in there fucking against the fridge freezer and I thought, bloody hell, the whole thing is going to topple over if they don't watch it. I went back in and Jon was lying on the floor squirting a tube on his chest going, 'Lube me up baby, lube me up!' and a woman in a mask with feathers on it just got astride Jon and started rocking backwards and forwards and laughing her head off. I filmed that for a bit and then I thought maybe I should join in, I thought, sod it, yeah, why not, that's what it's all about, it's a bloody free-for-all! So I put the camera down and knelt on the floor next to a couple and reached out and grabbed the woman's arse and came immediately and she goes,

'Piss off!' and Jon says, 'Oy, watch the carpet,' then started laughing so I thought I'd better go. But my clothes were all in the pile and a couple were on top of it so I had to try and pull my trousers out from under there, and I got someone else's shirt but it didn't matter, it fitted all right, I just wanted to go home really, and luckily I'd put my shoes and socks over in the corner, then I thought shit, keys, keys, so I had to go and try and find them, and right there was this bloke doing a woman doggy-style, and he was really going for it, but I had to tap him on the shoulder to get past and say, 'Excuse me,' and then had to look through the keys, thinking oh bloody hell because the bloke had stopped and was looking at me, just staring at me through the slits in his mask with glitter all over it, really giving me the evil he was, and the woman was looking at me as well because she was wondering why it had stopped, so I grabbed my keys as quickly as I could and went. I left the camcorder there because I thought Jon might want to look at the footage I'd done.

I shut the front door as quietly as I could so that they wouldn't hear me leave, and I could hear people moaning and laughing and someone slapped someone on the arse quite hard and they screamed out loud and someone else was going, 'Oh yes, *yes*,' and I thought, what will the neighbours think?

When I got to the car I realised I'd got the wrong keys, but I didn't want to go back and ring the bell so I walked home, it's a bit of a walk but I thought never mind, and on the way back I thought that next time I'll definitely wear a mask, and Jon can get someone else to do the videoing, I'm buggered if I'm doing it again.

the interview

I honestly did not think he would turn up, but I went along anyway. In case he did. He hadn't cancelled, not in so many words. Besides that, it had taken months to set the thing up. He rarely gave interviews. He wouldn't show, of course. His third wife had just killed herself, the night before. Some timing. He'd appeared at the gates of his mansion house up in the hills, on the news that morning. He'd looked like hell, like his world had been turned upside down, which, of course, it had.

The boss sent me out there anyway. Sure he did. 'What do you have to lose?' he said, and I couldn't give him an answer to that.

The interview was supposed to take place at 3p.m. at the Musso & Frank Grill. I'd booked a table. I asked at the door if my man had arrived.

I was directed to the bar that ran the length of the restaurant, with a view out on to the street behind it. It was bright outside, which made the bar gloomy and reassuring inside.

He was sitting there in the dark at the far end of the bar, tossing back a drink. There was a pile of crumpled paper napkins beside him at the bar.

I went over.

'I didn't think you'd make it.'

He turned and looked at me. If he looked like hell on the TV, standing by the gates to his mansion house, he looked worse now, worse than hell, if you can get worse than hell.

'Whu– ?'

'The interview.'

'Oh yeah, the interview,' he mumbled. He signalled the barman for another drink. 'You?' he asked.

'No. I . . . I'm sorry about your wife.'

'Why? It wasn't your fault.'

The barman topped up his glass and he slugged it down.

'If you'd prefer to do it another time.'

He shrugged.

'We're here now,' I said. 'Shall we take the table?'

'Prefer to stay close to the juice.' He pointed a finger towards the back of the bar, like he was pushing a button for an elevator.

I pulled out a barstool and sat down. 'Mind if I tape this?' I asked him.

He talked about his early career, how he used to work as a horse stuntman on westerns in the fifties, until he switched to acting in B-movies after breaking his collarbone. 'A lucky break,' he said. 'I literally fell into acting.' Then how his career had gone off the rails after a decade of boozing, fucking and fighting, and he had ended up on TV. Star of a long-running sci-fi show, which now, rediscovered on cable, had turned him into a cult star, and made him rich with repeat fees and tie-ins, festival appearances, and even a record.

He talked about his first wife, how the marriage had ended badly. He talked about his second wife; 'She was kinda cold, detached,' he said.

He didn't mention the third.

He'd gone to the men's room.

The barman came over and picked up the napkins and swabbed down the bar where he'd spilled his drink.

'Why don't you give him a break?' the barman said. 'He's took it hard.'

'I thought it might take his mind off it.'

'Why don't you just give him a break?'

He came back to the bar, walking slowly, unsteadily, and sat back down, signalled for another drink.

He sipped the drink, and said, 'She was the one, you know.'

'I beg your pardon?' I said.

'She was the one. She came along too late. We didn't want to grow old and grey. She didn't. No-one wants to grow old and grey.'

I didn't want to say anything. He looked worn out: he was *old*.

'You've had a good life,' I said.

'Exactly,' he said, straightening up from the bar. 'So much harder to leave behind. I've had it good, damned good.' He sunk the rest of the drink with a trembling hand. 'The poor – the miserable – they're the lucky ones. How sweet it is for them. But us – here,' he pointed out to the distance, 'up in the hills. We're doomed, damned. Finished. What's going to be waiting for us?' His eyes were watery, bloodshot. He seemed gripped by a genuine, unknowable fear. 'What's waiting for us?' he said again, his voice trailing off.

The barman came over and leaned down beside me and whispered in my ear, 'Why don't you just give him a break?'

There was threat in his voice; this was no longer a suggestion or request.

I paid for the drinks and left.

I typed it up and it came easy. It was a real choker.

Hollywood heartbreak, death in the hills. It was a beaut.

The boss chewed me out for the piece.

'You get the guy the day after his wife dies . . . and you bring me this?'

'That's an emotional piece.'

'It makes me want to cry. Sentimental crap. No-one wants to read about his career. Who in fuck's name wants to read about his career. Jesus. He was a lousy actor.'

'Did you ever see his early movies?'

'Come on. What happened to his wife? Why did she do it? What happened that night? You could have drawn him out. He'd have spilled his guts.'

'He was genuinely upset.'

'Sure he was. His comeback's taken a knock.'

'You going to run it?'

'Not like this. Maybe if you go back.'

'I'm not going back.'

'You're not, eh? What if I send you?'

'Then I go, and he doesn't answer the intercom at the gate, and I don't get to speak to him.'

'Well, I can't use this.'

'Well, that's a shame.'

'Ain't it just.'

Two weeks later he was dead.

Found face down in his swimming pool. Classic Hollywood death. He'd been drinking at Musso & Frank's every day during those two weeks, gone home and fallen in the pool.

The pool was shaped like a Martini glass.

They ran the story. Sure they did. An exclusive, his final interview. It sold plenty.

They showed one of his early films on television as a tribute. He was a very promising young actor.

He played an escaped convict who is gunned down by cops. His final line at the end of the movie was: 'Rather die here in the dust than rot in jail,' then he went for his gun.

luther's sickle

Luther had been building his motorcycle for so long, he couldn't remember how long, he'd forgotten that a long time ago, all he knew was that it was his *way out*. As soon as he got that thing started, which was any day now, he would get on it and ride out into the woods and never be seen again. That was his plan, plain and simple.

He'd been working on that thing for months, maybe a year. It was part Suzuki, part Kawasaki, part Moto Guzzi. Did that make it Kamikaze? Four hundred cc's, twin exhausts off a single welded downpipe, hardened steel shocks, front and back slicks. Boy, that thing was going to take off like a rocket, in Luther's opinion.

The reason Luther was building the bike was simple. He'd had it with everything and everyone, particularly everyone. It was time for him to move on, and that didn't mean get on a bus, or a train; it meant load up and move on. He was in a hurry to leave. But not that much of a hurry that he wasn't going to do it properly. It had taken him long enough to reach his decision that he was going to leave that he knew he ought to do it properly. Not sneak off in the night like he was sulking.

This way would be something different.

Each day and night that he worked on the bike, he was a step closer to getting out of there. He was close now, he could feel it. It was just fine-tuning now, surely.

That night he sat in the front room adjusting the fuel feed. Once the bike was no longer in pieces all over the ground and he'd fixed the oil leaks he'd moved the bike inside the house to work on it.

Once he'd done this, he thought, he could think about starting her up. Push down on the kick-start and . . . freedom.

He sat back and looked at the bike. It was a crazy, dirty-looking thing, but he was proud of it, its mismatched, rusted chrome body parts, its multicoloured panelling, the torn leather seat with foam sticking out, the rear wheel hub from a junked Jaguar, the low green welded frame which looked like a WWII messenger bike, and the icing on the cake, the ivory-tooled throttle handle with a wire running directly to the engine block. Where did he get the parts? Here, there and everywhere, that's where. From junkyards, scrapyards and backyards, he wasn't fussy, from abandoned vehicles left by the side of the road. If someone had a part he could use, he'd put it somewhere on that killer machine, no doubt about it. And that thing would go, he knew that much for free. It would go like a bat out of hell with a firecracker shoved up its ass. It would go like a – it didn't matter, it would go. He sat back and wiped his hands with an oily rag and thought, this is it, this is the moment. This was his moment, man and machine . . .

The sun had been coming up and Luther decided to rest. As he slept, he dreamed. He dreamed of riding along, the forest rising up on either side of him, a straight path ahead through the forest into blue. It was a good dream, it was as if he were floating. There was no sound, not even the sound of the bike. He felt at peace, which was unusual for his dreams, when he was usually being chased by some kind of yeti ape thing like his cousin Lyle said he saw, and his feet were getting stuck in the mud and he was running in slow motion, and all the time the yeti was getting closer; or were those nightmares?

Luther wheeled the bike out in front of the house. It was dark, and he planned to leave right there and then, end of story.

He looked out into the darkness, into the woods. That was where he was going. Deep into the woods and beyond.

Luther checked his pack was fastened tight on the back of the seat. There was nothing but essentials in there – a couple of T-shirts, wrench set, a stack of pornos and wooden nunchuks. Seeing the pack was secure, he got astride the bike and flipped the kick-start out with his hand. He put his foot on it and put his weight on it and kicked it over.

Once.

Twice.

Thrice times a goddamned lady!

The bike fired up the third time and he twisted the throttle, sending great blasts of noise into the night, the bike coughing and rattling beneath him.

Let this wake them up, he thought, let this blow them all to hell.

Luther kicked the gear down and let go of the clutch and the bike shot forward spraying gravel and dirt, the front wheel rearing up off the ground and wobbling from side to side. Luther leaned forward and pushed it down and opened up the throttle and the bike went clear through the perimeter fence and smashed both of Luther's knees, and he howled and twisted the throttle and the bike shuddered and rattled as if it was about to come apart at any second, but it was really moving now.

The woods were ahead, a pit of blackness, of darkness.

The bike disappeared and the woods swallowed up the

sound of the bike and Luther was gone, all he had left behind were bits of splintered fence all over the ground.

The bike ploughed on into the woods. Maybe I should have worn a crash helmet, Luther thought. The bike was bouncing all over the place, the low frame hitting the ground and zigzagging the machine through the darkness.

He tried to head in a plumb line, keeping the throttle twisted right down.

He'd drive until daybreak. Then keep on driving. He'd show those bastards. He'd show them *they* couldn't stop him, they couldn't stop anyone. *They* could say what they liked about what they liked and do what they liked, but in the morning *he'd* be gone and they wouldn't know where, and soon enough he'd send them a postcard and it would tell them all to go to hell and make no mistake about it. He would say I never did any of the stuff you said I did, I never sold no dope to no kids, they just said I did because they think I'm an idiot and I'd take it, and I never burned down the school just because I was seen round there that day when it happened, I never had no use for school, why would I give a damn about it?, and I never robbed the gas station, I wouldn't do that, I know Ted all my life and he'd been good to me, the only person who has, you think I'd do something like that to a friend, no sir, and now you can't say I did those things anyways, so I'll see you all in hell, is what he would write, if there was room on a postcard, and he thought that maybe he'd send a letter and have room to fit all of that in and some more even, but first things first . . .

Luther couldn't see too good and the front wheel caught a tree stump and the gears went and there was a terrible whine as the chain jammed and the cogs split. The back wheel flipped up, bucking Luther through the air.

Luther flew in an arc and hit a tree stump and was snapped in half and was killed instantly.

Should've rigged lights.

bones

My problem was that I always fell out of love with women. At first I'd be smitten, then a few months later, I don't know what had changed, I didn't seem to love them any more. Time and time again it happened, until it got to the point where I was waiting for it to happen each time and I'd wake up and sure enough I didn't love them any more, like someone had turned off a switch, and I'd think, well, here we go again. With the woman I eventually married, I was determined this wouldn't happen, and it was no coincidence that we had our honeymoon in the Caribbean island of _____. There, you see, they practise strange rituals – I had seen a documentary on television about it. Spells and so forth, voodoo. I sought out the foremost practitioner on the island . . .

One night, while my dear wife, whom I still loved, slept, I crept out of the hotel. A guide waiting in a jeep drove me up into the mountains. We parked and went the rest of the way on foot, deep into the jungle, into the darkness, until all we could hear were the bugs in the undergrowth. I wasn't frightened; I was full of love and followed my guide, eager for a cure to my errant emotions.

Soon we could hear drumming in the distance, the steady rhythm of a tribal drum, and we saw the glint of firelight and heard the occasional shriek. But rather than being filled with fear and trepidation and wanting to turn and run, I was filled with joy, and I thought of my dear wife, sleeping peacefully back at the hotel, and I said to myself, 'I'm doing this for you, darling, for us, for our love will be as others love, until the grave and even beyond, love unto eternity.' It was almost as if the spell had been worked already; I was entranced, and shivers of joy ran up and down my body.

We came through to a clearing and there, sitting by the fire, was a man with long white hair, his body painted, staring intently into the flames. He jerked his head to look at us as we emerged, then motioned me to sit at the other side of the fire, pointing with a stick hung with bones and beads and feathers and a beak. He shook the stick and his men came out of the shadows and gathered round him. I say I wasn't scared and I wasn't; I had an open mind and a loving heart. The men began to chant and wail and one of them fed the root and the flames burned up and out of control and the drum beat faster and I took off my clothes and the men smeared my body, and I leaped through the flames and grabbed the chicken stick and whooped and spun around, freeing myself, opening myself to the spell

'OOH-CHA-CHA-CHA-CHA'

until the stars exploded and love coursed through my veins.

I awoke back in the hotel the next morning, my body still smeared in the green and white paint, so I crept out of bed and showered and came back and looked at my wife, still asleep under the sheet, and I lifted it and her body had the contours of sand dunes and the calm of the ocean and I touched her and gently rolled her over and told her of my love and we made love – nothing needed to be said – we were both floating through space and time on LOVE.

I not only *loved* my wife, I lusted after her from that day on with a passion stronger than it had ever been before; it was teenage lust, innocent simplicity. I found no fault with my wife and was never tempted elsewhere, why should I be? Every time I set eyes upon her it was as if for the first time, and I made love to her at every opportunity, and when we weren't making love I gazed into her eyes. It was insane and unnatural, it was voodoo, but it was good, it was love, it was how it should be. And when I saw other couples it made my heart ache, because

I knew they didn't have the love we had. It was my wife I wanted, nothing more.

She fell ill. We saw a doctor and he didn't know what was wrong. She didn't get any better. We saw other doctors and specialists, but she became weak. I still made love to her, and I was gentle, more gentle than before, and tender, I still loved her and adored her, I was a man consumed by LOVE, and she was consumed by love. But she lost weight and became frail, ever so frail in my arms as I held her. No-one knew what caused it. She had no energy and became weak and often fainted, and I cried, how I wept, I knelt by her bed and held her thin white hand and pressed it to my face so that she could feel the tears. I sobbed and said, 'No, my love, my love,' and made love to her to prove my love, and my desire, and I promised I would look after her. It broke my heart that she wasn't getting any better; she was getting worse.

I knew it when it happened. We were making love and the life went out of her. I called the doctor and he came and told me, he told me she was dead.

She was my wife, I loved her, and I didn't want her to go, but they took her. I couldn't stand it, I had to see her, and I went to where they had her and I pleaded with them, please let me see her one more time, just to say my final goodbyes, and they left me with her and I made love to her but she looked cold and alone and it broke my heart. So we made love again. There is nothing better than being in love and for that love to last, and our love would last, and then I heard someone coming.

Later I had to make arrangements for the funeral and they asked me, 'Do you want the body cremated?' and I said, 'God, no!' and before the service I was given some time alone with her, and I climbed up into the coffin and lay with her and we made love there, one last act of love before she was in the grave. When they lowered the coffin into the ground it was all I could do to stop myself jumping in there after her.

The weeks and months passed. I couldn't bear to be apart from her, I couldn't stand it, so I went to the graveyard with a shovel and I dug, I dug up the grave, and I got in the coffin and by now she was just bones, and I knew I'd get caught, but you can't stop this kind of love, you can't put brakes on love, and eventually they came and dragged me out by the ankles, and I was grabbing at her and I said, 'At least let me keep the SKULL!' and the vicar shouted, 'God, man, what's got into you?' and I said, 'LOVE!'

Now I'm in a cell, and they won't let me out, they say it's a crime, they say the things that I've done are crimes, and I say how can it be a crime, to love your wife? That was all I did, I loved her, and I still love her, and that's a crime?

They can't see that, they don't know love; if they did, they'd have let me keep the skull, or some of the bones at least.

music

It was when the music came on that I became uncomfortable and eventually had to say something. Call it music, I found the noise offensive. *Teen Bliss*, I think it was, I don't care to remember.

'Could we – do we have to listen to this?' I said.

'Whoah – my friend . . . my house, my rules.'

Indeed, it was rude of me, presumptuous even. I was a guest for dinner and a guest should go some way to accepting the host's taste in music. Call it what you like. To my ears it was diabolical. I actually found it painful. I just couldn't stand it.

I reached into my jacket pocket and took out the disc.

'Put this on,' I said.

He stared at the disc and his wife stared at the disc in silence, silence except for the music in the background, if you call it music, which I only do for the purposes of description.

'Try it,' I said, handing the disc to him.

He took hold of the disc by the edge and considered it. His wife narrowed her eyes, looking at him. Then, good-naturedly, he got up from the table and went over to the hi-fi.

He stopped his 'music', replaced his disc with mine, then lingered for a moment, and, looking over his shoulder, said, 'This isn't . . .?' then shook his head and pressed play.

It was almost inaudible at first, but it was there, and soon it filled the room and we were all flung back in our chairs as if hit by a physical force.

He rang me a couple of days later.

'You have to tell me where I can get that disc,' he said.

'You won't be able to get it in a shop,' I told him.

'What is it? Mail order or something?'

'It'll take some time.'

'Then do me a copy.'

'A duplicate?'

'Yes.'

'A duplicate won't sound . . .'

'To hell with that! I haven't been able to listen to anything else. It's killing me. I put on another disc, it's like a fucking headache. Even the music in the lift makes me

want to vomit. That stuff – I mean, Maria too. She wants
me to get the disc.'

'I can't –'

'Please, please do me a copy, for me –'

'OK.'

'Soon.'

'And what the hell is that disc anyway?'

'Well –'

'Forget it.'

He hung up.

I knew how he felt. Once you had heard that stuff, well,
you couldn't listen to anything else, you just couldn't. It
was as if you were having trouble sleeping, and had been
prescribed sleeping pills and then could never get to sleep
again without them. I should never have played the disc to
them in the first place. They wouldn't thank me for it.

He called up a few days later.

'Jesus, man, did you do my copy?'

'Look – like I said . . .'

'Don't "like I said" me – Maria's in bed with her ears
stuffed with cotton wool, in case she hears so much as an
advertising jingle. Christ, I was stuck in a traffic jam,
some guy pulls up alongside – he's playing that teen-
anthem bullshit – that "let's everyone get together"
bullshit. My brain nearly fucking exploded. My ears

started bleeding, right there in the car. Actual blood coming out of my fucking ears. I can't turn on the radio, I can't do anything. Someone hums a fucking tune they might just as well whack me in the back of my head with a cricket bat. GET ME THAT FUCKING MUSIC!'

'I'll come over,' I said.

The music finished and we sat there, the last waves flowing over us.

They lay back on the couch, holding each other. Maria had tears streaming down her face.

'Beautiful,' she said, 'beautiful.'

'Oh *fuck* –' he moaned.

He fell forward on to his knees and clasped his hands together until his knuckles whitened.

'Please,' he said, saliva bubbling on his lips. 'Please – you have to let me have that disc. Please.'

I didn't answer. He moved his hands as if to go for my throat, then, realising what he was doing, checked himself.

'You FUCK! Didn't you know what you were doing to us?'

'I should never have –'

'But you did – you did . . .'

Pause.

'If I give you the disc –'

'Don't fuck us around any further, or I swear –'

'*OK*, OK. I'll let you hold on to it.'

Maria let out a wail of exhausted delight.

'It's OK,' I said.

He fell at my feet and clutched my ankle.

'Thank you, thank you, thank you.'

They took Frank and Maria in a couple of weeks later, confirming what I already knew – that I should never have given them the disc. They didn't know how to be discreet. They had a dinner party, twelve people, and put on the disc. Jesus Christ, it had taken me six months before I played it to anyone, and even then . . . but a dinner party! One of the guests didn't care for this flagrant disregard for regulations, and reported them. It didn't help in any case that Frank was turning up to the office with his ears bleeding. Dead giveaway.

Luckily the trail didn't lead back to me. But my supplier cut me off dead, and it had taken me years to find a reliable supplier, would take years again.

Of course, they'll try and find out where Frank and Maria got the disc. They'll strap them into a chair and play them music until their eardrums are perforated like someone is sticking a lit cigarette into them. They put stuff on like *Teen Bliss* and *Trippy Baby*. You've just got to hold out until you can't hear any more. I only hope that they hold out.

from your son, jorge

Yes, mamma, it is true. I finally got into Oxford. Oxford English Language School on Tottenham Court Road, where I make planning to improve my English language skills. Don't worry for me, mamma, I have a new friend who is security man. He say he watch my ass.

It is really wonderful, I have many new friends, mamma. London is full with all types of people. My work-mates are from faraway places like Trinidad, Jamaica, Antigua and Kilburn. I met a real Londoners as well, mamma, but they speak Greek and I no understand them.

I am working now at the BBC (British Broadcasting House) and have very good job. They have made me head in charge of Channel 2, in charge of all the programmes like *Dad's Army*. They pay me two pounds and fifty pence every hour. I think soon I will be able to afford to take a beautiful girl out and find a wife. I lie, mamma, I work in canteen but I see a lot of white pussy every day.

I live in a bedsit apartment with a sink/urinal and view of the locomotive yard. You know how I love the trains, mamma, and the sound of the choo-choo, which I hear every morning as the crow flies. There are hookers next door and sometimes they give me suck. Tell grandma hello.

One evening I take a stroll in Soho, and people shout things at me, mamma, but I think they are jealous of the leather trousers I buy in Carnaby Road with my payslips.

Oh mamma, I fear I will be seeing you, papa and grandpapa, grandmamma, sooner than I think. They caught me doing to the cleaning lady what I did to Julio's donkey that time, only this time I didn't have to put honey on it to get her to lick it and now they give me the sack.

Oh mamma, you know I tell you about my friend Angelo, the security man, well he try to kiss me, mamma, so I no longer have any friends in London.

Oh mamma, will nothing go right for me in the land of wine and roses? I am evicted from the bedsit for partying with the hookers. I pay them, sorry mamma, and they suck me good until the landlord find out.

Good news, mamma. I have another job, thank the Lord Jesus. I give out leaflets for the Oxford English Language School on Tottenham Court Road. I make lots of friends and sometimes I throw the leaflets in the bin and go to McDonald's. They do the nuggets, it is just like back home.

I have move in with Angelo. He not so bad. We have made it up, mamma, now we share the rent and plenty else besides.

Ah mamma, you and papa must visit, London is wonderful, just like the Austin Powers movie, you remember, mamma?

Write me, mamma.

P.O.W.

When Yan never came back, I says to myself, I'll come and find you, I'll get you out of whatever motherfucking bamboo cage they've got you in. I thought, he was only ever coming back in pieces, in a body bag, missing an arm, or a leg, an eye out, limping with a stick; either that or they had him in a bamboo cage, out there in the jungle, half-lowered in water, the bastards, so there would be fungus growing off his feet. I know those bastards, those motherfucker zips, they'll keep ahold of Yan as long as they please – and for what purpose? There are many, many of our boys still out there, prisoners, and they say the only reason those bastards keep hold of them is for 'leverage', in case war breaks out again. And we've said, time and time again, that as long as they have got hold of our boys, then we are still at war with those fucking animals. But hell, what is the government doing about it? Sweet fucking nothing. They deny there are still prisoners. I say, keep denying it, but I don't see Yan at the bar on a Saturday night, and I don't see Yan breaking chairs over some guy's head just because he is wearing a cowboy hat, and Yan saying, 'I hate country'; no, it's not happening. For the particular reason that Yan never did come back. And they say, 'He's dead,' and I say, 'Show me his dog-tags,' or any part of him for that matter. And they can't. So I say, to hell with it, I'll go find Yan myself. And that's exactly what I did.

Been eight years now. War been over eight years. Eight years after the war I come looking for Yan. Won't go home without him.

When the plane touches down it all comes rushing back, and the heat, Christ, I think, how did we ever fight in this heat?

I go straight into the city from the airport, and book into a hotel. It ain't much but it will do. I think, goddamn, was there ever a war in this town? There are people walking along the street like nothing ever happened. And I know that Yan is out there somewhere, and others, and these people walk around like they don't have a care in the world. Well, I do care. I'm gonna find Yan, and bring him back, and any other poor bastards I find along the way. Hell, there might be a bunch of them in a cage, in which case they're all coming back with me. Fly the boys back home and march up to Washington and present the motherfucking president with a bill, saying, this is how much it cost to fly these boys back from fighting the war, your war, and we didn't even fly first class. Yes, that will be a proud moment. Show those fuckers a thing or two about patriotism.

First thing I do is get myself a whore, Mai Ling, or Chang Ching, or Wang Chun, or something. Get her to come up to my room. As I remember it, those girls will do anything, and that means everything with a little bit more sprinkled on top. Those girls know more tricks than motherfucking Marvin the Magician. So I get her in the room, and point to Don Johnson and say, 'Earn your three American dollars'; only language they understand.

I'm holed up there for three days, with Chai-Ling, whatever her name is, and I'm damned if I'm not worn out by the end of it. I don't get much sleep, and that is not because of the noise from the traffic on the street outside all through the night, no sir.

I figure it is about time to get moving on the Yan situation, because, like the Chinks say, 'Walls don't paint themselves.' And for all I know, Yan could be out there right now having bamboo slivers shoved under his toenails, and I figure Chai-Ling is as good an 'in' as any; she's connected, she tells me her cousin can get me just about anything I want, and that would be a high-powered assault rifle, bolt cutters and some grenades, maps, and directions to the motherfucking place where our boys are being held. Money no object, a dollar goes a long way here. She arranges a meet.

Well, this boy surely did come up with the goods. I forgot how good this shit tasted. Damn near blows your head off after a couple of hits. Shit. I lay back on the bed and thought the ceiling fan was a chopper, like in the movie, rolled off the bed and hid under it. When I heard Mai Ling coming down the hall, goddamn, if I'd had an M-60 I would have blown her head clean off. You don't lose the survival instinct, that is for certain. You might get flabby round the gut, but you do not get flabby round the head.

Shit, where am I?

Dreamed I was in the jungle there, night patrol, I'm walking point. Can hear Yan crying out in the distance. Sounds like they're working him over real good. We're trying to get near him but he just gets further away, all the time, the jungle just seems to be getting thicker and thicker, sucking us down. Yan is screaming now, it's ringing in our ears, and I shout out, 'We're coming for you Yan,' and all of a sudden all the leaves and branches part and we're surrounded by grinning gooks pointing their bayonets at us, and I put my hands up but they move in, and about twenty bayonets go into me, I wake up screaming, covered in sweat, breathing hard. I think, that was it, a cry for help, Yan calling me. Don't you worry, Yan, I whisper. I reached and grabbed what was left of a joint from the ashtray on the floor by the bed. I lit it and smoked it down. It relaxed me good. I went back to sleep.

Yes sir, that weed is mighty effective shit. I tell Chai-Ling, tell your cousin to get me some more of that shit, money is no object, and how is he coming along with the marching dust we soldiers are so keen on? She says that I should not keep mentioning I was a soldier in the war, that it upsets her people, and I say, 'Hellfire, it's the stone-cold truth, why hide from reality? You can no more hide from reality than you can from a tracer coming at you out of the sky. I ain't ashamed.' And I take another hit off the joint. These fuckers got a problem with the Stars and Stripes, well, that is their problem, not mine.

We go out and meet the man again, I tell Mai Ling to go on ahead, I'll meet her there, and just for the hell of it, I wear my green army shirt, with my name on the front, and the Stars and Stripes on the side. Man, you should have seen their faces when I show up at the Tee Kee bar wearing that, but I say, 'Do not worry, I come in peace,' and hold up the victory sign.

Mai Ling comes over and says, I think we should leave, and I say, hell no, I just got here. Well, I buy all those boys a drink, and I can tell, it does not sit easy with them, and only by about the third round do they seem to not mind me buying the drinks. I don't drink too much, ordinarily, but hell, that Jack and C was slipping down fine. Well, after a while, I figure, it was time to liven the shit up, and I say, 'I hear you fuckers like to play Russian roulette, who's got a gun?' and put my finger to the side of my head and go 'click' with the thumb. Well, Mai Ling is pissed and starts tugging at my arm, and I say, 'Nothing personal fellas, nothing personal about what you boys did to our boys, I heard all about it. Say, I got to take a leak, the crapper ain't booby-wired is it?' Well, I head off to the head, and I'm standing there pissing when fucking ying and yang come in and stand either side of me at the trough, and I think they want to take a piss also, but instead they grab me and force me up against the wall. I say, 'What, gonna torture me now? You'll get nothing out of me, hear? Nothing!' and they say, 'We don't like what you come here for,' and I say, 'Hey fuckheads, if you've got something to hide, then I'm gonna find your asses out, if you've got our boys, I intend to find 'em, try and stop me. You got beef with that?' and one guy says, 'No, you coming here to fuck our women,' and the other one knees me right in the Hanoi Hiltons and I go down.

I wake up with a faceful of piss and go looking for Mai Ling.

*

That bitch has gone AWOL, so all I have for company in the hotel room is a big bag of buds and Uncle Jack and Uncle Daniels. It gets to the point where I go stir crazy, dancing round the 12 by 12 in cammo underpants, putting my fist in the mirror, all that shit, the way troops go out there, any sound of slants and it is forward roll into the bathroom and hide behind the shower curtain, lights out, purple vision. Those fucks are everywhere and they want a piece of me, and they don't care which piece.

One time there is a hammering on the door, sounds like mortar fire. They slip a note under the door, 'Will call back'. Like I'm gonna stay to find out what for. I put on the full regimental and slip out down the fire escape.

End up in a bar, tossing 'em back, till I get loud, saying 'Goddamn Ba Muoi Ba, ain't you got Bud?' then the barman starts ignoring me, I shout out, 'Fuck you, fuck you, Charlie don't serve,' like in the movie. Out on the street three of those rice-munchers jump me – I say, 'There's three of you and only one of me – bring it on,' and they kick the shit out of me, a regular rat fuck.

Get back to the hotel, figure it's got to be safer there, Mai Ling is in the room, going through my shit, cammo gear everywhere. She's holding up my passport, saying, 'Did not know you Dutch, thought you Yan-kee.' I say, 'Fuck you mai-leene, whatchoo doin' with my shit?' and she says, 'I bought you more shit,' and waves a goddamned baggy. 'Make you feel better.'

I say to her, 'That's not all I need, sister, I need some tender lovin',' and pull out a roll of notes, tell her to go round up a dozen fine chickens, and bring 'em back here toot-sweet, to mission control, for some patrolling of enemy territory.

Well, she comes back with the women all right; twelve of 'em lining up outside the hotel room door, and I let 'em in one by one, then two at a time, threes, and I send Mai Ling out for some more shit, so I can keep this fuck-festival going on strong. What goes on behind closed doors, well, let's just say, I was halfway to fucking half the female population in Saigon in half. Gets to the point, the manager is hammering on the door, and I'm saying, 'What you want?' and he says, 'I want in! I want in!' and I says, 'You want some?' I send Mai Ling to talk to him; she tells me he wants me out, they need the room, and I say, 'No way, get more women, get more shit, the party has just started,' and she says, 'The room is booked for someone else, they need the room back,' and I say, 'GET!' I give her more money. I say, 'Pay the room, get the women up here.'

Manager keeps ringing the phone in the room, banging on the door, says, 'This no brothel, customers complain, need room.' I say, 'I ain't leaving, you think I'm goin' out on the street, there's people want my ass,' and he says, 'No-one want your ass, I want your ass out of room,' and I say, 'KISS my ass.' Gets so I won't let the girls out of the room, case he gets the idea of coming in. I say, Mai Ling, she's the only one that comes and goes. Then the manager only goes and shuts off the electric in the room, that fuckhead zip mo-fo. Think we need electric to fuck and get high? Since when? Never did, and don't. Besides, we got candles. Hot without those fucking fans though. I send Mai Ling out for ice, and say, 'Use the fire escape.' She says, 'OK, Dutchman,' and I say, 'Cut that shit out and go.'

Been there what, how long? Weeks. Don't know if it's day or night. The manager is knocking on the door real loud, shouting, 'This is your last chance, then there real trouble,' and I hear his footsteps going off down the hall, and think, fuck him, he's fucking dinky dow is all, and say, 'What's he gonna do, room's paid ain't it? Fine way he treats us for getting him free.' Mai Ling says, 'Get who free?' and I say, 'The war baby, the WAR!' and she says, 'Did you fight in the war?' and I say, 'Fuck has that got to do with it?'

Can't be more than an hour later, people shouting outside on the street like something is up, then there's a big noise coming down the hall, and all the girls stop what they are doing, and it all goes silent for a second then all of a sudden the goddamned door comes off its hinges, and I'm fucked if the place don't fill right up with smoke, a bunch of fucking gooks come out of the fog, military I swear, shouting and pointing guns and shit, so I shout out, 'Let's roll,' and the women are all crying out, and those fuckers are on me, hitting me with gun butts and trying to keep me down, but I say, 'Boys, you will have to do better than that,' and they pull me off the bed and hit me with some kind of electric prod in the side and I stiffen up and keel over. They stick a rubber gag in my mouth and strap me onto a gurney, all the time shouting crazy shit I can't understand. I can't see shit for the smoke and all of a sudden I'm lifted up and out of there.

Well, they ship me out of Saigon as quick as they can. Guy from the embassy says to me, 'We know why you are here in Saigon and we do not approve of what you are doing.' So I say, 'Hell, I only bin havin' some fun, foolin' around with the women and all, and look where that got me, and besides, half that shit is legal anyway,' but they say, 'No, we mean about looking for prisoner-of-war camps,' and I say, 'Shit, I forgot all about that.'

‘p.o.w.’

Glossary

Ba Muoi Ba	Vietnamese beer
dinky dow	Vietnamese for 'crazy'
gurney	wheeled stretcher
M-60	US machine gun
point	lookout who walks ahead on patrol
purple vision	night vision
rat fuck	doomed mission
tracer	chemically treated bullet that glows en route to target
zip, gook, slant, Charlie	derogatory terms for Vietnamese national

the incredible doctor octor

Doctor Octor was the worst doctor on Harley Street, yet, perversely, one of the most successful. He was not a properly qualified doctor in the first place and this was something of his appeal.

Octor treated his patients appallingly; his female patients were subject to a barrage of degradations on every visit, that much was guaranteed. A woman complaining of a sore throat might be told to take all her clothes off.

'For a sore throat?' she would ask Doctor Octor.

'Come on, hurry up, I haven't got all day – take all your clothes off and put them in a pile on the floor next to mine,' Doctor Octor would say, sitting at his desk, perfectly naked, smoking a pipe.

On one occasion, a woman suffering from headaches was told to strip and do a handstand in front of a full-length mirror. Octor then placed his head between her legs and looked at himself in the mirror.

'Well, doctor?' the woman said.

'Mmm,' Doctor Octor replied, stroking the pubic hair where his chin was rested. 'The boys at the squash club were right – I would look stupid with a beard. Now, what did you say the problem was?'

How Doctor Octor came to set up his practice, unqualified, why his patients stood for it and, furthermore, why he became a success, will be revealed forthwith.

At first his patients were shocked and appalled by his antics, and threatened lawsuits. They murmured of 'putting him out of business' and 'damage claims'. However, when it became apparent what was involved with such a lawsuit; well, it was one thing to tell half a dozen dinner-party guests about Doctor Octor's method of 'oral administration', for example, but quite another to tell a court of law. The newspapers would have a field day. The patients didn't care to demolish their own reputations, simply the doctor's. The planned lawsuits were quickly withdrawn. Anybody who asked, 'What happened with that dreadful Doctor Octor business?' would be told it had been settled out of court. Of course, it hadn't been at all. Octor never paid a penny. And, more than likely, the patient would book another appointment.

The thing was, his clients came to enjoy his

outrageous diagnoses. Traditional medicine was so dull compared to Octor's methods. You never knew what he might do next. His reputation became such that soon it was difficult to get an appointment. People who weren't even ill would come for a check-up. He was taking on new patients every day of the week.

Not just women, but men too; men who would be bent over the examination table, and 'examined', after which Octor would snap off his surgical gloves and exclaim, 'I could have sworn I left my keys in there somewhere.'

How on earth could such a practice exist? Simple. Octor rented a premises on Harley Street, put a sign on the door, and waited, quite confidently, for patients to arrive. It was, of course, the address that did it, and the difficulty in getting an appointment to see a doctor on Harley Street. When people discovered they could get an appointment with Octor, soon he was busy also.

How did this medical deviant come to be a 'doctor' in the first place? He wasn't always a 'doctor'. He was once a 'lawyer'. He took an initial consultation fee but never, ever took on a single client. Before that he ran a dating agency with the slogan 'Only the beautiful need apply'. The private clinic, though, was proving his most lucrative endeavour so far.

Well, of course, you want to hear about the downfall of Doctor Octor. We'll come to that.

On the afternoon a year to the day after the surgery had opened, Octor had just finished inspecting the breasts of a beautiful young woman. She was worried that her implants might have been leaking. The doctor had spent twelve minutes fondling the ripe young chicken's firm thirty-two double Ds, before letting out a cry of ectasy and releasing his hold on the bosoms.

'Any leakage?' the girl said, fastening her brassière.

'Yes, but not from the implants,' Octor said, going back behind his desk in a half-crouch. He sat back down and wrote out a prescription, which he handed to the girl.

'WILL YOU MARRY ME?' he had written on the slip of paper. The girl blushed, buttoned up her shirt and left the examination room.

Octor, quite pleased with that one, called in the next patient. That being the rather tragic figure of Cleckley, a health authority regulator passing himself off as a temporary patient in order to check on Doctor Octor's medical practices. No-one knew such regulators existed. Doctors presumed that six years in medical school was adequate preparation for diagnosing haemorrhoids and so forth. Doctor Octor, on the other hand, considered a bronze plaque on a Harley Street premises ample qualification for the job.

Cleckley was a small, insignificant man, with a half-formed moustache and a worn-out tweed suit. He was overly anxious, prone to ulcers, eczema, and often down with the flu. It was the perfect job for him; unlike most regulators, he didn't have to invent an ailment when he went about his undercover work. He was usually suffering from something. If the doctor was not able to diagnose and cure the stomach cramps or skin complaint, Cleckley thought to himself, Cleckley might just as well have him struck off the books as incompetent.

'Sit down, sit down,' Doctor Octor told Cleckley, then asked, 'You don't mind if I sit on your lap?'

Cleckley was quite startled as Doctor Octor positioned himself on his lap and said, 'What seems to be the problem?'

'Legs – aching,' Cleckley gasped.

'Yes – well – rheumatism?'

'No – you're sitting on me!'

'Ah, yes, of course, I must lose some weight,' the doctor said, jumped up and began pacing the room, brushing the back of his head and rubbing his chin. He then went up and stood close to Cleckley and said, 'So, what's the matter?'

Cleckley, his face reddening, said, 'Big toe – HURTS!'

'Aha! Arthritis? Yes?'

'YOU'RE STANDING ON MY FOOT!'

'Clumsy of me,' Octor said, and resumed pacing back and forth.

'The thing is,' Cleckley said, 'I'm suffering from

depression. I feel all alone, isolated from society. People ignore me, I –'

'Nurse, send in the next patient,' Octor called out.

'You see, doctor,' Cleckley said, and Octor, turning to Cleckley said, 'I'm a doctor, not a psychologist, I can't help you with *that*. Don't you have any physical ailments?'

'Well, I –'

'Never mind. Drop your trousers.'

'I beg your pardon?'

'Do as I say.' Octor motioned him to proceed with his disrobing.

'I don't understand.'

'You're not supposed to, I'M the doctor,' Octor declared, pointing a finger to the ceiling. 'It's just routine.'

Cleckley began to unfasten his belt, while Octor turned to his desk, slipped on a pair of surgical gloves, then undid the catches on a small black leather case on the desk surface. He removed from the velvet lining of the case a small silver-handled object with an eye-piece and a thin metal tube attached at the top. He turned around to face Cleckley.

'Remove the underpants also,' Octor demanded. He noticed Cleckley nervously eyeing the silver instrument in his hand.

'Ah this. Brand new! A revelation in the field. It's a urethrascope. Marvellous for prostate complaints I'm told. Spots them before they happen.'

Beads of sweat formed on Cleckley's brow.

'Underpants,' Octor said, moving forward.

Cleckley coyly pulled down his pants. He looked away as Octor knelt before him peering through the urethrascope; anticipating excruciating pain, Cleckley tensed his body. What happened instead might be considered worse.

'It really is quite the smallest thing I've ever seen,' Octor exclaimed. 'Tiny, absolutely minute. That such a miniature thing could serve such an important function – yet so utterly minuscule!' Octor began to titter.

Cleckley pushed Octor away, pulled up his pants and trousers, and stood there with them bunched around his waist.

'I've never been so insulted,' he said, his voice quavering and cracking. 'This is a disgrace!'

'Upset . . . insulted,' Doctor Octor said, quite mystified. 'Why on earth –?'

'How could you say things like that to a *patient*?'

'Oh yes, I see. No, I was referring to the urethrascope. You must admit it is so small, yet the task it performs . . .'

'You were NOT talking about THAT . . .'

'Nonsense, nonsense,' Octor said, patting Cleckley on the shoulder. 'Nothing for you to worry about in the waterworks department, I can assure you. A clean bill of health. You'll make somebody, somewhere, very happy, someday. Sit yourself down, and don't fuss.'

Cleckley, regaining his composure, sat down in the chair.

Octor replaced the urethrascope in its case and turned once more to face Cleckley, who was busy tucking in his shirt.

'Nothing else wrong with you?' Octor asked.

'Not that I –'

Before he could finish, Octor grabbed Cleckley by his nose, twisted it, yanked it, in short, mangled it, so that when he pulled his hand away it looked like nothing more than a huge strawberry.

'I've got some cream for that,' Doctor Octor said.

'Yarr-oo!' Cleckley cried out, grasping his nose. He got off his chair, tripped and sprawled on the carpet, scrabbling towards the door.

'Nurse, nurse!' Doctor Octor called out, as he pinned Cleckley to the floor.

A slim, extremely attractive nurse entered, dressed in a neatly pressed light blue medical uniform with a watch hanging upside down on the left breast pocket.

'This man is hysterical,' he shouted. 'Bring me a shot.'

When Cleckley came to, the nurse was sitting next to him on the doctor's couch, her soft breast pushed against his arm as she leaned forward to put a thermometer in his mouth. He felt a cool flannel on his forehead. Cleckley felt altogether more relaxed than he had done in a long time.

'A mild case of hypertension,' Doctor Octor said, sitting at his desk writing out a prescription. 'Stress in the workplace no doubt. What is it that you do?'

'Uhm – ah – gubberment . . . in – spector,' Cleckley mumbled, as the nurse took the thermometer out.

'A slight temperature,' she said.

'Yes. You need a rest cure,' Octor said. 'Simple as that. Take some time off immediately.'

The nurse removed the flannel from his brow, and helped Cleckley off the couch.

'Meantime, have one of these, twice a day, after meals,' Octor said, handing him the prescription.

'Thank you, doctor,' Cleckley said, quite forgetting why he'd come there in the first place, and left.

'Send in the next patient,' Doctor Octor told the nurse.

'She hasn't arrived yet,' the nurse said.

'In which case, take *your* clothes off,' Doctor Octor said, and started to remove his own.

the singer

Every morning when I get up I sit at my dressing table and look in the mirror and say to myself, 'I am what I am, no-one can stop me, no-one can change me!' That's what this business is all about, self-confidence. You've got to have self-confidence, got to believe in yourself. You've got to have a sense of humour as well, otherwise you'd go mad. So I look in the mirror and say, 'Look at yourself, you wrinkled old thing, who do you think you are, you're thirty-six years old, do you think you're going to make it?' and I answer myself back, 'Nothing's going to stop me from making it!' That was the way my ex used to speak to me, but not quite as nicely as that. When we rowed he'd say, 'Why don't you jack it in, you silly cow, you're making a fool of yourself, you're over the hill.' And I would say to him, 'What about Jayne MacDonald off the telly? She was on the cruise ships, look at her, she's sold millions of records, thousands,' and he would say, 'She looks like the back end of a boat and can't sing so maybe you have got a chance.' I said, people would have told her she was past it, and if she'd listened to them, she would never have got anywhere, but she didn't listen, and look at her now, she's got her own TV show, with men dancing and lifting her up, and he would say, 'Well then, why don't you piss off on the cruise ships then?' So that's what I did, and it's the best thing I've ever done. You've got to start somewhere, so I did, and I think of Jayne, and I say, 'I can make it,' because I was starting to get scared I wouldn't make it, because time was running out. But look at Robbie Williams – he started at Butlin's, I think, as a Redcoat, and he was an alcoholic and *he* made it.

I'm enjoying this cruise more than anything, but I'm not getting on too well with the head of entertainments. I haven't worked with him before and he can be a bit testy. I arrived a bit late at the Emerald Room tonight and he started on at me, saying that all the musicians and dancers were there on time, what made me so special, and who did I think I was, Jayne MacDonald? He knows I like her because I told him when we first met that it was my ambition to be the next Jayne MacDonald and he's used that against me ever since. The thing is I don't like to get there too early before my set, because a lot of the musicians and dancers are smokers, and that can affect my voice, all that cigarette smoke, I don't like it. I said to him, 'I don't want a throat infection,' and he said, 'Come off it dear, they wouldn't know the difference if there was a bullfrog up there singing,' which I thought was a bit of a rude way to talk about the audience, after all, they are paying our wages, and they pay good money to hear the entertainments. I mean, it is all included in the package, but it's the show that sells the cruises, especially after Jayne MacDonald, a lot of people come hoping they're going to see the next Jayne MacDonald.

I love the buzz of performing, it's better than sex, it's better than anything. To get up there on the stage in front of the crowd and hold their attention like that, and do songs they recognise, I wouldn't swap it for anything. I love the audience, I love their enthusiasm, I love to see them entertained and I love to be the one entertaining them. When you get a good audience, there's a real connection, you can feel it. Some nights I look out and see a sea of faces, and because they are a lot older, they remember the show tunes, the show-stoppers, and some of them just close their eyes and lie back in their chairs and let their heads drop back and enjoy the music. Sometimes they don't clap, not all of them, because they've been carried away by the music, like they are in a trance.

Tonight there weren't many people in because apparently they were doing a two-for-one at the Flamingo

Room – but I was glad in a way, because it meant I could save myself for tomorrow night. Tomorrow night is the Emerald Room gala showcase, basically the big entertainment night on the cruise, the night before we dock for the first big excursion. I had something special planned, and the head of ents had agreed to it. It was just as well I saved my energy tonight because some of the passengers, who must have been at the two-for-ones, came in and started shouting and ruined it for everyone else.

It's funny being aboard a ship, anything can happen. Sometimes I wake up in the night and think, where am I? Then I remember, I'm in my cabin, on the ship, and I go back to sleep. Sometimes I dream that I'm drowning, and my lungs are filling with saltwater and it's black, and then I wake up and I can't breathe. But it's not the drowning I'm worried about, it's the not being able to sing! I don't know what I would do if I couldn't sing. I live for music. My ex said he reckoned there must be something wrong with me the way I went on about music the whole time and said, 'My life is music,' but I don't care what he thinks, I just felt sorry for him that he couldn't understand. Anyway, it doesn't matter now, I've washed that man right out of my hair! And there have been plenty of fellas on the ship who've shown an interest in me, bought me a drink after the show and been perfectly charming. You never know when there is a possibility of romance onboard. There are always new faces on every trip, new passengers and staff. I had a bit of a thing with the purser a few years back, but he disappeared when we got to Puerto Balleros. Afterwards I found out he'd been accused of stealing money from the ship's accounts, so that must have been why he went off like that without saying anything.

I went for a drink Monday night, after the show, just the one, mind, so I could wind down before the big night! This fellow approached me at the bar and said, 'You're the singer,' and I said, 'Yes.' 'I heard you tonight,' he said, 'why do you sing?' So I said to him, 'I love singing, singing is everything to me, it's my life, it always has been ever since I was a little girl and I used to sing into a hairbrush . . .' but he said, 'No, why do you *bother* singing?' then started laughing and walked off, and I thought, I bet he's one of the lot that had been at the two-for-ones, I bet he was the one who shouted out, 'Harpoon her!' when I came on stage. I should have known he was drunk from the way he was swaying when he was talking to me, but I thought it was just the motion of the ship. I thought that he was just plain rude. I don't know why people feel the need to say things like that, it was just hurtful. But like I said, you've got to be tough in this game, thick-skinned, skin tough as a rhino, because, heaven knows, I'll have to take a lot worse than that where I'm going, and that is all the way to the top.

It will take more than a jealous little man to knock me down. I'm going for gold!

I put on my red dress, the one with the spangles on it, which I save for special occasions, and an imitation diamond choker and earrings. I'd had my hair done specially – we get a 50 per cent discount at the salon, so I thought I'd take advantage of that – and I thought I looked smashing. In fact, before I went out I looked at myself in the mirror and said to myself, 'You do look good in that dress, girl, don't listen to what anyone says,' like my ex who said, 'You look like a fucking glitterball, they ought to hang you from the middle of the ceiling and spin you round.' But he would have eaten his words. I'd slimmed down a lot since then, I did the Lorraine Kelly calorie castaway course and now the dress looked like it was made for me.

It was time to go down there. I was really nervous and excited and thinking, you go for it girl. But as I was walking along the walkway, ever so carefully in my heels because it gets wet and slippy, one of the cabin doors swung open all of a sudden, and knocked me on my backside. A man came out of the cabin, the chef I think it was, shouting and waving a bottle around, and a voice from inside the cabin shouted, 'Piss off, you fat queer.' The chef went off down the walkway, and I thought, charming, don't help a lady in distress, and when I did get up I had an oil stain on my bottom and I thought, just my luck, that's a nice start, but it was too late to go back and change.

The Flamingo Room had been closed for the night especially for the gala. When I arrived they told me that the place was packed, so I got even more excited and forgot all about falling over.

The head of ents was backstage, all dressed up, wearing a bow tie, being ever so nice to everyone. I think he was as nervous as we all were. He even came up to me and said, 'You go out there and knock them dead.' I said to him, 'Is it OK if I do my special number?' and he told me, 'Well, OK, if you get an encore you can. Have you told the band what it is?' and I said to him, 'I told you before, I'm doing it unaccompanied,' and he goes, 'Oh yes, what is it?' and I went, 'It's a surprise.' 'OK, good luck,' he said, and I said, 'You're not supposed to say that, it's bad luck,' so he went, 'Break a leg,' and I laughed and said, 'I nearly did that already.'

After the dancers had gone on to open the gala I peeked round the curtain to look out into the audience. I could see the captain was there, and the ents manager had joined him, but there was someone else there I didn't recognise, and I thought, maybe he's an agent! Then my heart went all into a flutter. I'm terrible with nerves but I only need to get out there and start belting the songs out and they disappear just like that.

Before I knew it, it was my turn to go on. I couldn't believe the applause, it was wonderful, and I really fed off that energy, I felt so thrilled, it's what every performer dreams of. I went on, hit my spot and was careful not to turn round in case they saw the stain on my bum, just nodded to the band and they started and off we went.

Oh, it was wonderful. There was no way of explaining it; it was like being a seagull, flying out over the ocean, soaring. The audience loved it, they were cheering and clapping, and I had to wipe a tear away from my eye. I did my three songs and after the third one they kept on clapping, I was on a tremendous high, then I saw the head of ents give me the thumbs up so I knew it was OK to do my special number. 'I'd like to dedicate this song to Jayne, my inspiration, Jayne MacDonald, ladies and gentlemen,' and they clapped some more. Then the stage lights dimmed and they put a spotlight on me, I waited a moment, and then started to sing.

The practice had paid off, and my voice held, right up to those high notes, it was as clear as glass, and it felt like I was walking on air. It was as good as her version of the original version, the best I have ever sung, and by the time I got to the end of the song I felt a tingling sensation all over my body – *here, there, every – where* – and when I stopped, there was silence, a silence that seemed to last for an eternity. My heart was pounding, my arm was outstretched, and it felt like I was the only person in the room. Then the light came up slightly, and the audience were looking at me. Some of them were shaking their heads. I heard this tutting noise and looked over to the wings – it was the ents manager waving at me from the side of the stage. I didn't know what was going on, so I went over to him and he pulled me off the stage really roughly and said, 'What the fuck do you think you're doing?' and I said, 'What?' almost crying now, and he said, 'It was hardly fucking appropriate to sing the theme from *Titanic* was it?'

I don't know what to do now, he made me feel ashamed. I daren't leave my cabin, I'm sure people will be talking about it. I don't know why I did it, I just thought it would be a nice song. I wouldn't have done it if I'd realised.

Luckily everyone's got something different to talk about now because apparently someone fell down a stairwell and broke their neck or something so maybe they'll stop going on about me. I've got half a mind to get off and fly home when we get into port, but then everyone would go, 'I told you so,' when I got back. To top it all, I think I'm losing my voice. But that's what this business is like, it's like anything else, you have good days, you have bad days, but you just have to keep on, and don't let anything get in the way of your dreams.

the indian

The stripper was up there on the apron stage doing her stuff, all the moves, underneath an arch of multicoloured balloons, but with a look on her face that said she didn't care too much for it, she could take it or leave it. This got the man, sat at his table with a little lamp on it, a few rows away, drinking his beer, this got him more excited because of course she was above all this, she was better than this. She was a terrific-looking girl, a knockout body, great tits (real, he was certain), and now all she was wearing was glass high heels and a garter to slip dollar-bill tips into. He didn't even notice the other girl, who was still wearing silver panties, twirling round on the pole in the middle of the stage behind her.

The music was hitting now, he thought it was quite the greatest tune he had ever heard, and as she gyrated her glorious backside and swung her hair and spun around, grabbing her breasts, he thought it was really the best tune anyone could think of for dancing to in this situation. He thought, you have not lived until you've seen a great-looking girl, with wonderful tits and ass and a shaved pussy dancing to this. It was like a religious experience! Why did they do that, why did they shave their pussies like that? It drove him crazy! A thrilling, maddening, tingling sensation, like an electric insect, ran at speed down the length of his spine and disappeared through the seat of the chair and the moment was gone.

He slumped, momentarily, then got up, and went towards the toilets, glancing as he went at the mean-looking Indian on the door, who looked like he might chop your hand off at the wrist if you so much as touched one of the girls. A big bastard, with long jet-black hair tied into a braid that hung neatly down his back. A big, mean-looking bastard.

He locked himself into a cubicle and proceeded to put white powder up his nose. The white talc is for those who can afford it, he thought. Why then, in order to administer the stuff, did one always end up in a toilet cubicle? Such a sordid experience. He took the snuff and marched back in.

The music was still going, that same great tune, that fucking music. He clenched his fists tight by his side.

The lap-dancer was at the edge of the stage, kneeling

down and leaning forward, giving a little show to the guy sat there on his own, right next to the stage, with a Scotch and a stack of dollar bills on the table beside him.

What was wrong with the guy? Was he fucking blind that he needed to get that close? His face would be in her tits in a minute, then the Indian would chop off his fucking head.

He went back to his chair and sat down.

I'll give her a dollar, he thought. Nothing wrong with that. Show my appreciation.

He stared at those tits. He liked the way they moved as she danced. They didn't swing, or sway, they jumped on the spot.

He took a dollar bill and folded it lengthways, then in half. Such was the fashion.

He got up and walked to the stage. Each step measured and awkward. It was like he had a limp, then he missed a step and thought, keep it together bigshot, everyone's watching.

She looked at him approaching. He managed a weak smile. She turned side on and lifted the leg with the garter band; a small rosette of dollar bills fanned out beneath the elastic. She pulled the garter away from her thigh and he slid the note in, his forefinger brushing her soft, tanned skin for just a second. He glanced at the Indian who was frisking someone down at the door. That fucking hump! If he'd seen that he'd have snapped me in half, he thought.

The girl mouthed 'thankyou'.

He nodded his head, turned and went and sat back down.

After she'd finished her dance, he requested a private friction dance with the girl.

She led him into a small, dark, mirrored room, sat him down and motioned him to move his knees apart.

He gave her twenty dollars. She smiled, tucked the note away, and began to undress. She had to dance to whatever music the girl on stage had chosen. Madonna or some such shit. It didn't matter.

Soon, she was totally naked again, standing between his legs, grinding her backside into his crotch. The mirrored walls reflected the scene into eternity on both sides. He stared downwards at that beautiful rear end, and felt his hardness, and looked away and saw himself in the mirror, helpless, pressing himself back against the wall as if someone were trying to get past him. He reached and loosened his collar and tie, felt the first vestiges of panic crawl up on him, and thought, soon I will have some more talc. He took several deep breaths, stared down again, then placed a hand on one of her buttocks. He thought it was wonderfully firm. She kept moving, so he put his other hand on the other buttock . . . still nothing. So he started plumping the buttocks, the way one would a pillow, then leaned forward so that his body was pressing against her back, cupped a hand on her breast, gently squeezed, and felt it respond. All of a sudden the Indian was on him from out of nowhere, had him up against the wall, his hand around his neck, squeezing. His feet were off the floor, kicking, like he'd hanged himself. The Indian must have been eight feet tall. The girl was cowering against the other wall, trying to cover herself, staring up at him. Had she signalled the Indian? Or had the Indian seen by chance? He had to believe that she hadn't minded what he'd done.

The Indian was screaming at him, but he couldn't hear too well, and the Indian's big hand was tightening around his neck, and he could feel the blood trapped in his face and his eyes misting over.

He was dragged out through the club, thrown through the doors and landed violently on the pavement, rolled to the kerb and knocked his head against the wheel arch of a jeep, setting off the alarm.

The Indian stood at the door, watching him.

The man got to his feet and staggered away down the street, then turned and said, 'I'm coming back with a baseball bat and I'll take your fucking head off.'

The Indian slammed the door shut and went back in.

He crouched down behind a car that was parked on the other side of the road from the club. It was six-fifteen in the morning and the sun was up, and he stayed out of sight in case a car went past or the Indian saw him.

I should have wrapped some barbed wire around the bat, he thought, as a special treat.

No sign of his girl yet, or the Indian. A few of the girls had come out already and the last of the bums inside had gone home. Even the manager, that fat greasy pop-eyed fuck, well, he'd left, so he knew it was closing-up time. Maybe he'd left that fucking Indian mopping out the crappers and the overgrown knucklehead was in there licking the remnants of coke off the toilet tanks.

He waited some more.

The snuff powders had worn off by now. Making him feel half-dead and worn-out and impatient.

Fuck that! he thought.

I'll kill that son-of-a-bitch. Son-of-a-fucking-squaw.

He grabbed the bat, and, swinging it from side to side, crossed the street to the doors of the club and went in.

He stopped in the reception area. It was dark in there, no-one around, the smell of beer, cigarettes and disinfectant in the air. Barstools upturned on the bar.

Music was playing. Like nothing they'd played all night. Some kind of 'do – dee – dee – dee, do – dee – dee – dee . . .' thing. A ballad. Cranberries or some shit. He felt a pulse down his spine. He moved along the wall into view of the stage. A single light was on, a spotlight aimed at a glitterball in the middle of the room, spinning round, throwing tiny silver specks all over the walls.

In the middle of the floor in front of the stage, the

tables and chairs had been pushed back to form a small circular space. The girl was there, in jeans and T-shirt, slow-dancing with the Indian.

She had her head rested on the Indian's chest; his head was tilted forward mournfully.

The Indian heard the baseball bat drop to the floor, but when he looked up the man was gone.

The Indian locked the doors to the club, and they started walking home.

Someday, someday soon, he said to himself, I will get us out of this fucking town.

You have to be tough in this life, bullet-proof, he reminded himself.

Someday she might leave me, he thought, looking down at his girl, and you have to be prepared for that.

Some slick Rick might come and take her away from all this.

He looked up at the sky and thought, today it might rain.

They walked on.

the swamp

Lyle Talbot crouched down in amongst the mangroves there, where it was cool and the breeze was coming in off the water. The river came up over his ankles but it didn't matter to him. He'd been in the swamp three days now, and it had got to the point where the mosquitoes didn't bother him any more, he didn't even swat them away, just let them settle on him until they got bored and left of their own accord.

He took off his hat and wiped his forehead with his forearm. He rubbed his eyes and looked out.

It was gloomy in there, and still. He could hear birds in the distance. And occasionally, far, far off, the sound of a truck up on Alligator Alley.

He'd worked his way up north from Monroe over the past three days. Now he was much further north than where he'd seen the thing the first time. He knew it was out there and he was going to find it. He was going to prove it. He'd keep going until he found it. Hell, he'd go clear on up into Kissimmee if needs be, it didn't matter. If he had to eat sawgrass for food, and drink the river water, he'd do it, until he found that thing.

The reason he knew it was out there was that he'd seen it before, with his own eyes, not twenty feet away from him.

He'd been out on the scenic trail east of Monroe, checking that no-one had laid any bait on or around the paths so that no animals would come close to the visitors. That was his job, essentially; National Preserves paid him to do that.

It was late afternoon and the tourist bus had just left, the tourists taking pictures of alligators and shit, when he'd seen it, out there in the trees, looked like some kind of a big shadow. It was standing there stock-still when he first noticed it, and he didn't know what to make of the thing, and then it started moving, just walking along like you or me, and damn near scared the wits out of him. He knew it wasn't no bear, no sir. What bear walks along like that? No bear he knew, unless it was a performing bear, the kind they once had over in Naples, and then it would have had a hat on, but he didn't see no hat. He didn't start following the thing immediately, being as he was frozen paralysed with fright, and so when he did start after it at a distance, the creature was pretty soon out of sight. He could just hear it crashing through some trees until there was no more noise.

Now, of course, what he should have done there and then, which would have been the sensible thing, was to have gathered some evidence, for example, got a camera and taken photographs of the footprints the thing left and so forth, so that he might have proof of what he had just seen, this sight that he himself couldn't quite believe. That's what he should have done, instead of go whooping down to Everglades City to Joe's and run in the bar-room shouting, 'I seen it, I seen the skunk ape!' Everyone just waved him away and got back to their beers, because they knew Lyle Talbot, he was always telling one story or another, like the time the alligator bit the wheel of his jeep, which everyone knew was a story from years back he'd stolen off the fire chief anyway; no-one had forgotten, particularly the fire chief, who got pretty pissed when he heard Lyle was telling that story and passing it off as his own, and said to Lyle, 'You know the alligator bit my jeep, Lyle.'

'No, I did see it,' Lyle went on, pointing and jumping up and down. 'Out there in the woods!'

'There's us thinking you saw it at Mitch's deli counter!' Joe, behind the bar, said, setting Lyle up a beer. 'Settle down, Lyle. Everyone knows that thing don't exist. Brings the tourists in is all. Only people do believe is tourists, some of 'em, and Indians, and even they ain't sure. Hell, I'm half-Cherokee, and *I* don't believe it.'

'You would if you saw it, Joe, that's all,' Lyle said.

'Lyle, are you sure it wasn't someone dressed up in an ape suit? Rudy maybe? Are you sure you and Rudy didn't go over to Naples and hire yourselves an ape suit from the costume shop?'

'If I'd have gone to the trouble of hiring an ape suit, don't you think I would have got a photograph of the goddamn critter? Besides, I don't talk to Rudy much any more, on account of that business with the shirt.' Lyle claimed Rudy owed him money for a new shirt after his shirt got torn by Rudy. Rudy claimed it was torn by accident as a result of a tussle between the two of them after they had been drinking one afternoon, so it was no-one's fault. Lyle told him to pay half and Rudy told him to whistle for it, and they'd fallen out over that.

An old-timer at the bar had piped up, 'Cop in Broward claimed to have seen the thing in seventy-seven. Turns out he was drunk on duty. He used it as an excuse for being drunk. Said, "I need a drink after seeing that thing out there on the highway, to calm my nerves." Claimed it ran out in front of the car. Took his badge.'

'The ape took his badge?' Lyle asked.

'Not the ape!' the old-timer said.

'Why would I make it up?' Lyle asked. 'I did see it.

Hell, it even smelled. It smelled rotten like stinking eggs.'

'Your story stinks,' Joe said.

'It's certainly rotten,' the old-timer said.

Lyle got drunk that night, drunk as a skunk ape, because no-one believed him and it was frustrating for him to have seen that damn thing but have no evidence. What was the point of that? At the end of a long night in Joe's bar he proclaimed, 'I lied about the alligator biting the wheel on my jeep, I admit that now, but I'm not lying about this!'

It didn't get any better. People around town started making fun of him after that; he couldn't go anywhere without someone commenting on it. It got so they were saying some pretty hurtful things like, 'I seen something big an' hairy in the woods, Lyle, I think it was your mamma havin' a lie down!' Then he lost his job as a result of the National Preserve holding an official line that the Bigfoot did not exist; they didn't want one of their staff going around telling everyone he ran into on the nature trails that he'd seen an ape, out there in the swamp. Why, it would make them a laughing-stock if they employed someone like that. Part of the reason he lost his job was because he was neglecting his duties, spending more and more time away from the trails, searching the swamp, looking for that ape. He argued his case that they had to find the creature before it did any harm to the visitors, but the Preserve was of the opinion that it hadn't done anything yet, nor was it likely to, seeing as it didn't exist. More to the point, the only harm that anyone had come to recently was when a tourist party was chased by a wild boar and if Lyle had been spending a bit more time concentrating on his job he might have been able to prevent that.

So it was all or nothing now for Lyle. He had nothing to lose, he had to find that creature now; his livelihood, his reputation, depended on it. Heck, even his old man had kicked him out of the house, saying, 'No son of mine is going to go around town acting crazy and bringing the family name into disrepute,' to which Lyle replied, 'No, that's your job.' But Lyle suspected that the reason his old man had reacted like that was because Lyle had taken to drinking quite a little since the incident and his old man didn't react too kindly to Lyle helping himself very liberally to his liquor supply. Besides that, getting drunk and challenging his old man to a wrestling match more often than not resulted in a chair getting broken and someone getting hit with a chair leg.

So, Lyle had taken his old man's hunting rifle and a knapsack of bare essentials, which included rope, rubber water socks, and a short length of stick in case things went hand-to-hand, and headed off into the swamp to find the ape. If, and when, he found the thing, he had no choice, he was going to have to shoot it and tie it up and drag it back to town and display it there in the town square for all to see. He'd be in the papers and on TV. They loved a story like that.

But the moment seemed far off right then, crouched by a tree, the rifle across his knees, waiting for another night to close in. He figured he'd go out and find a bit of dry copse to sleep on until daybreak. It sure wasn't comfortable sleeping out in the swamp, and Lyle was getting tired as hell, not getting enough sleep. But it beat sleeping on Rudy's couch, the way he had been since his old man threw him out, and having to listen to Rudy snore like a buzzsaw in the next room. He had almost gone next door and put a pillow over Rudy's head. At least the swamp was quiet. Apart from that noise he'd heard the night before. He thought it might be the creature, beckoning him deeper into the woods. It had sounded like a mating call, a wild screeching noise followed by a chattering and a high-pitched squeal. Then he thought, what if the creature comes for me, and wants my cornhole! and wished he was back on Rudy's couch. But then sometimes he had the suspicion that *Rudy* wanted his cornhole; it was just a thought, but Rudy did live all alone and never showed much interest in girls, even when Lyle had shown him dirty pictures when he was a kid, come to think of it. Sometimes Lyle would lie on the couch and think, Jesus, he might sneak in here one night and then what would I do? The only reason he stayed at Rudy's was because he figured Rudy still owed him for the shirt, and could repay him this way. Besides, he had no other place to go, like in the movie where the marine is doing press-ups and being squirted with a water hose and he says, '*I got no place else to go!*'

He only wished he could track the seven-foot fleabag down sooner rather than later. He only hoped he wouldn't have to go into Kissimmee after all. There were no trails there, the swamp was thick, and it was just the sort of place where the thing might hide and not be found. Lyle started to wish that he'd never seen the damn ape in the first place, but then he started to realise he must have seen it for a reason, and the reason wasn't so he could try and forget all about it and pretend it never happened, just because the folks in town treated him like a fool.

He felt sorry for himself. What did they know anyway? Who were they to say that it didn't exist? Things went on in the swamps that they didn't even know about. All kinds of things. Burial grounds, bodies. What if he'd walked across sacred ground? The Indians wouldn't be too pleased about that. It got him shivering just thinking like that, all alone out there, walking on graves. They could bury him in the swamp and no-one would know, no-one would care, apart from the fella he owed money on his jeep to, but he could probably claim the insurance. Lyle tried to get himself to stop thinking like that. He wasn't alone – there were creatures all around. He'd seen bobcats and alligators and one time he thought he might have seen a panther. Sometimes he felt there were eyes on him, because of course the creatures saw him, but they knew he belonged there, he was a native, this was his home as well as theirs. But really he just wanted to stop walking and start blubbering, but he didn't, he just kept going because he knew if he did start blubbering, that would be it. He had to keep it together.

The next day, he considered, he would go across Alligator Alley, and into the Kissimmee Swamp. He'd never in his life been further than Alligator Alley, why he'd never even been much further out of Collier County. People was always going on about how the Glades were being destroyed, way he saw it, there was plenty left of them; you could live your whole life and not see the whole swamp or know what went on in it.

He heard a 'gator splash in the distance and some birds taking flight and leaned his head back against a mossy tree trunk. Something touched his neck. He turned about and it got its hands around his neck, and forced him down, and he struggled and a shot rang out but the rifle was aimed high and wide. He tried to cry out but the damn thing was crushing his windpipe, and he thought, why did I not smell it? Thing smells awful. But then he figured, three days in the swamp and you don't smell too good yourself.

'EE-AA-OO-OO!' the thing went.

Strangled to death in the swamp by an ape, he thought – now would they believe me?

He woke up lying face down in the swamp with his head in the weeds. He rolled himself over and stared up at the branches overhead. It was morning. His neck ached like a damned thing.

Slowly, he got up and out of the water. His daddy's gun was broken into bits, which were sticking out of the swamp. There would be hell to pay for that. His knapsack had been thrown up a tree and was hanging from a branch, the contents spilled out in the water underneath. He put the palm of his hand to the side of his neck. He would sooner have died than have this happen. That filthy ape playing hide-and-go-seek. He was going to look an even bigger fool now. 'I saw the ape again and it strangled me this time.' He tried to jump and get the knapsack but it was too high, so he had to get a stick to try and get it down. He felt a fool, out there in the swamp doing that. He started to sob, and stood there blubbering for a while, and when he was done blubbering he picked up his things and started off south, back towards Monroe.

he sees us

I'd been Jimmy's mechanic for a couple of months up until then; I was over working as a service mechanic for Porsche all over California. Before that I'd worked the racing circuit in Europe for a number of years.

I first met Jimmy at a race meet over in San Bernadino. He had a Porsche Speedster then. I'd been introduced to him as a Porsche mechanic. He won the race that time. He was a good driver, he had a feel for the road.

Jimmy got in touch with me a few weeks after that. He'd bought himself a Porsche Spyder that he wanted me to look over. I told him I'd be more than happy to.

It was a grey teardrop Porsche with one-fifty on the dial. That was a beautiful car.

Earlier that week, an actor friend of Jimmy's had seen him with the car outside a restaurant in Santa Monica, and had said to him that Jimmy was going to die in that car. He said, 'You know you're going to die on the road if you drive that car?' Jimmy said people always acted like that, it was natural, it was a fast car and Jimmy liked to drive fast, he loved to race. People were always worried, they were always saying, 'You're going to kill yourself.' His bosses at the studio banned him from racing while he was shooting a movie, and they were never happy about him racing.

Jimmy was a big star then, so it was no surprise that everyone got nervous about what he did, and watched his every move, and tried to look after him. It only made Jimmy want to do it more. He didn't like to be told what to do. From what I heard, Jimmy used to get up to all sorts, not just car-racing, but other stuff that his bosses at the studio, and his fans, would not have liked even a little. But it was the racing that really did it for Jimmy.

When it happened, we were driving along Highway 41 out of Paso Robles. We were headed to a road race in Salinas. Jimmy was going to compete; he'd just finished a movie. He was really gunning the thing, so I said to him, 'Jimmy, save it for the race.'

Jimmy looked kind of crazy that day, sat behind the wheel, and I don't say that because of what happened, not at all. His hair was all grey from the movie he'd just finished where they'd made him up to look like an old man. And there he was, this crazy old man hunched up behind the wheel of a sports car, driving along at top speed.

I saw a car up ahead on the intersection about to turn. Jimmy saw it too. It was way ahead of us but the speed we were going we'd be on him pretty soon. I said to Jimmy to slow down, and Jimmy said, 'It'll be all right, he'll see us.'

It all went into slow-motion, like a movie. Jimmy didn't even touch the brakes, but it all slowed down. I guess we just clipped the front of the car on Jimmy's side, but that was enough. There was a terrible noise, a sudden rush of noise, a roar, and Jimmy disappeared.

Jimmy didn't stand much of a chance. He was dead before they got him to the hospital. The newspapers reported me as being 'seriously injured'. Funnily enough, the guy we ran into, the guy who pulled out into the road, well he was pretty much OK, apart from being a bit shaken up by the whole thing. I was thrown free of the car, but Jimmy, they had to pull Jimmy out. The car was a total wreck. It was only a small thing in the first place, but now it was just a crumpled-up bit of metal. Minutes before, I'd been talking to Jimmy, and he'd been real excited about the race, he'd been waiting all that time to race – it was like the acting and the movies and all that stuff was just something he did in between racing. He was so excited he could barely wait to get there.

People acted pretty strange around me after the accident, after I got out of the hospital, which was quite a long time after. I got the feeling that they wished that if anyone had survived why couldn't it have been Jimmy? After all, what was I? I was just a mechanic and there's plenty of them. They took to looking at me odd, as if they were measuring me up to what Jimmy used to be, and it was always no contest. Soon, people didn't talk much about the accident, although I've been told they talked about it a hell of a lot right after it happened, but by the time I came out of hospital it had died down a bit.

Every now and then it comes up, and people find out I was in the car with Jimmy and they say, 'Oh no, the passenger died,' or, 'I thought he was in the car on his own,' and people say, 'How does anyone know what his last words were?' and I say I heard him say them, I was there that day when the twilight drowned out a grey car with a driver with silvery hair driving at 130mph; I was there when he narrowed his eyes and stared out through the windshield and didn't slow down. I say I was there when I heard Jimmy say his last words and they ask, 'What were his last words?' and I say, 'He sees us.'

I was there because I heard him.

plastic ape tits

The first time I saw Joseph's kid, I'm ashamed to say, was at the christening. God knows, I should have got round there sooner and seen the child, but I hadn't got my shit together to do it. I suppose, in a way, that I was reluctant to go round there, and see the kid, and Joseph, and his wife, the house, the nursery. Shit! That meant it was all over. We were not kids any more, we hadn't been for a long time, but why face up to that? It is a bitter pill to swallow, and seeing a kid in a cot is the only way, I guess, to swallow that pill down. As a race we cling to youth and all that it involves, for dear life, as if it were our last hope. I know I did. Take, for example, the night before the christening. I'd been out boozing my head off, drinking until 3a.m. at some godforsaken hole. I awoke with a fearsome hangover, the terrible terrors – did I do, did I say? Didn't – who . . .? The terrors that could only be calmed with a drink, but I awoke late and had to hurry to get dressed and get over to Joseph's, where, I thought, there would be plenty of booze flowing to wet the baby's head, and I would feel better for it. For God knows, I was worth less than nothing with the dry horrors making my skin crawl, and clamming up my jaw so that I couldn't speak sense but was awful self-conscious, jumping at slamming doors, excruciatingly ill at ease. Indeed, on the drive over there I could only peer over the steering wheel like a reluctant soldier ordered out of the trenches. But the first drink, if I could get it steadily to my lips, well, the resuscitating powers of that would be immediate and extraordinary. The colour would flush back into my cheeks, and my mood would change from morbid fear and mournfulness into a warm, comfortable glow.

But, arriving at Joseph's, I felt the weight of horror on me, and as I parked the car and approached the front door of the house, and heard the noise from within, I nearly buckled, but thought, no, onwards, this is Joseph's family's day, not mine, they won't give a flying fig about me, they won't even notice me, I should just get in there and mix into the crowd, get the drink down me and then enjoy what follows. This was a day for celebration.

Joseph opened the door for me and beckoned me in, and we hugged the way old friends do, then he led the way through to the front room, where his family and his wife's family and friends were huddled tight around the cot. Joseph said, 'Here, let me get you a drink,' and grabbed me a flute of Buck's Fizz, and I thought, mercy hallelujah and reached out a trembling hand, and I thought if I grab that thing it is going to go everywhere (and there is nothing I can do about that). But then Joseph said, 'Wait a minute, what am I thinking of? You haven't seen the baby yet,' and snatched the glass away and put it down. I was thankful for that, if only because it saved me from that awkward shaky behaviour. He pushed through the huddle and I followed, everyone muttering and murmuring and cooing, and a couple of fishwife friends of Joseph's wife acknowledged me coolly. Then Joseph said, 'There he is, there's my boy,' and I peered into the cot, and there, swaddled up in a blue blanket, was a pair of hairy plastic fake ape tits, the kind that you'd find in a trick shop.

'Ain't he cute?' Joseph said. I looked up and his wife looked at me coyly, and the grandparents looked down in delight.

I looked back in the cot and at the plastic ape tits, and scratched my head and rubbed at my eyes, my heart racing ever so slightly, and I thought, what occurs?

'Do you think he looks like his old man?' Joseph said, and I looked at him, then down at the hairy ape tits and all I could think of was to say, 'He's got more hair!'

'Thank God!' Joseph's wife said, then reached and

picked up the ape tits and cradled them and everyone went, 'Aaahhh.'

Except for me. My mouth had dried out and I certainly needed that drink, but we were all hemmed in, in a knot around Joseph's wife and the pair of plastic ape tits being rocked back and forth.

'Son, I need the toilet,' Joseph's dad said, and started to move out of the huddle. I took the opportunity to follow, and as I did, and we got clear of the cluster of folks, I noticed that Joseph's father had a pair of plastic ape buttock cheeks sticking out the back of his trousers. The trousers had in fact been tailored such that they accommodated the protruding brown plastic butt cheeks. I had to look again and watch him as he rounded the corner and left the room. I turned and looked at Joseph who was still with his wife cradling the hairy plastic ape tits.

Christ, where is that drink? I thought, and went and grabbed one from the mantelpiece and gulped it down. Oh mother earth, I thought, and took another drink, and stood there leaning against the mantle, drinking them down until I felt calmed. But sure enough, Joseph's father came back from the toilet and walked past, and I looked down, peering through my fingers where my hand was rested on my brow, and those shiny plastic cheeks were still in place.

Oh Christ, I thought. Are there nibbles? Perhaps I needed to eat.

No, I thought. This is wrong. Something is out of joint. I couldn't stand here, while they were over there . . .

I drained the glass and went back over to the huddle.

'Let me hold him,' someone was saying.

'No, let me hold him,' someone else said.

Really I felt that *I* should hold him, because that would put a stop to it, to this charade; but I felt bad about doing that, because one should not hold a child in the state I was in. I would advise against it; the poor mite's life is in your hands.

But I barged forward and grabbed the child and brought it to my chest. But it was not a child, it was plastic ape tits, fake novelty tits and hairy!

They all gasped and Joseph said, 'What are you doing, mate?'

I held the plastic tits out and shook the sheet off. It even had the elastic attached that goes round the back to hold the ape tits on when you wear them, dangling down like an umbilical cord. 'This – is fucking bullshit – this is not a child – this is fake plastic ape tits. I have been brought here under false pretences.'

'He's mad,' Joseph's mother said.

'Give me the child,' Joseph's wife said.

'Give me the child,' Joseph said.

'Give him the child,' Joseph's father said.

'You can talk,' I said, clutching the hairy ape tits. 'You

have fake plastic ape buttocks. Look, see for yourself. Show them your plastic butt.'

He looked from side to side and shrugged.

'Show yourself!' I shouted.

'Easy now,' Joseph said, and reached and took hold of the plastic ape tits.

I relinquished my grip on that thing, that abomination, that novelty-store malediction.

I was breathing heavily and slumped against the wall. Everyone glanced at each other and cast disapproving looks.

'Look,' I said. 'Look at his plastic buttocks. Touch them!'

Joseph had handed the plastic ape tits to his wife and her family moved in and closed rank around them. Joseph took me by the arm and hurried me out of there. He opened the door, and we went out on to the front steps.

'That thing in there,' I said. 'Those plastic ape tits. That is not a child, Joseph, that is not a kid.'

'Go home,' Joseph said, 'because you've already ruined the day.'

My impulse was to slap him, slap some fucking sense into him, but I restrained myself.

'Joseph —'

'What is wrong with you?' he said.

'Wrong with me? Your kid is plastic ape tits.'

'That's it. Get out of here.'

I turned and walked up the path to my car. When I reached the driver's side door I turned round and said, 'One day, Joseph, you will thank me. You'll thank me because I told you that your kid is plastic ape tits.'

'And to think,' Joseph sneered, 'we were going to ask you to be the godfather.' He went back inside and shut the door.

I got into the car and drove home, only weaving slightly.

orson beadle, travelling salesman

Orson Beadle, carrying a small briefcase, wearing a long mackintosh coat, stopped on the pavement, early evening in balmy summer, outside a pub on the corner of the street.

Despite the raucous noise from within, of men, alcoholled, watching football, screaming and shouting, jeering and cheering, a general air of violence and unpleasantness, Beadle pushed the door and went in.

Inside the pub was a crowd of the worst scum on the planet. They had been there for the best part of the day, drinking and waiting, the way these men do, unloved wretches, noisy foul-mouthed apemen, worth less than nothing to anyone. To their employers (those who had them) they were a mere liability; in the eyes of their spouses (those who had managed to retain them), they were hateful, unpleasant villains, quite brave enough to beat up a woman if their impulses dictated it. To anyone who passed them on the street, they exuded, quite naturally, menace, intimidation. In short, they were everything that was bad about their race, the human race. But anything must have its best and its worst, and if they didn't exist, then another worst would replace them, so they might as well be. They were best cooped up in their pub, together, and truly horrible. The landlord tolerated them as long as they kept drinking and wrecked the place a maximum of only twice a month. The big flat-screen TV did something to hypnotise and placate them. He kept a length of pipe behind the bar.

Beadle bypassed the bar and walked around in front of the crowd, standing, sitting, huddling round the TV showing the game, and stood in front of them and the screen, not obscuring it exactly, but certainly diverting their attention towards him.

'Now, gentlemen,' he said, as he placed his case on the floor and unbuttoned his coat, drawing out two large, fleshy, eighteen-inch dildos, once in each hand, drawn from the pockets in the lining of the coat; one jet-black, the other pink, both rubbery and smooth to the touch. The room went quiet, apart from the sound of the TV.

'Who'd like to have a go?' he asked.

'You fucking ponce!' one of the crowd shouted out and lunged at him. Beadle dealt him a swift blow with the black rubbery cock, thwacking it across his face. It did little more than stun the man, but it was a rude shock and he stood still for a moment, then sat back down.

'You fucking cunt,' another man said, standing up. Indeed, the whole crowd seemed to lurch forward.

'Now please, gentlemen.' Still gripping the rubber dildos, Beadle opened his jacket wide. Attached to Velcro straps in the lining on both sides were all manner of dildos and vibrators. He even wore a necklace made of multicoloured love beads. The men eased back and fell silent. 'Doesn't that set the mood? Gentlemen, I will explain why I am here. This is an opportunity for you all to try any of the items you see here, completely free. And believe me when I tell you, you will not believe the results.'

'Oy!' It was the landlord.

'You might want to try also,' Beadle said, and held up one of the rubber cocks, and jiggled it. The landlord scowled.

'Bring me a Scotch,' Beadle said. 'And make it a double – I'll need a double.'

The crowd bristled, but with uncertainty, shifting about uncomfortably in their seats. They were ready to jump Beadle, to bundle this man into the corner and club him to a pulp with broken chair legs. But none of them wanted to receive a lashing in the face with a rubber cock. A beating was a beating, but a man coming at you with a rubber cock was something different altogether. A rubber cock in the face was unthinkable. The man who had received one was still rubbing his face in confusion. The crowd eyed each other and thought, shall we try and bring him down? Should we? Or will we receive cock in the face for our sins? It was beyond them to get the measure of Beadle, a man who would do as he had done; there was nothing obvious about what he had done, and no obvious solution to the situation.

Beadle carried on.

'Once you've shoved one of these beauties up your arse, you'll know it's the way. There will be no going back. Think of it. No more trouble with women for one thing. Think of that!'

There was a murmur of consent.

'Which of you gentlemen would like to try out, for example, this fremula clamp? Combined with a regular vibrator and some lube, it can provide quite an effect.'

'Oy, cunt – we're watching the fucking match,' one of them said, but it was certainly half-hearted, a guarded plea that would not warrant an assault with a rubber nodule.

'Gentlemen, please, do as you like, but this is a very serious offer. There really is no obligation. The manufacturers are so assured of the quality of their product that they are prepared to make this offer. There are no hidden catches. There's even one here that squirts yoghurt that is available for demonstration.' Beadle put down the dildos he was holding and snapped the catches on his briefcase. He opened it and took out a red box. 'Who'd like to try this?'

There was silence, again. Only the sound of the TV, and a chair scraping the floor.

'Just think, gentlemen. Consider for a moment the possibilities. No more sound than that of an electric razor.'

Someone jumped up. A small man with badly receding hair, wearing a football top. 'I'll fucking — I'll fucking —' His face was red, and he looked ready to smash something. 'I'll fucking buy one!'

'You're welcome to try it first,' Beadle said.

'Just fucking give me the thing,' he said, grabbing the box and running off towards the toilets.

There was a pause, but soon people were waving twenties in the air.

'Steady gentlemen,' Beadle said. '. . . and read the instructions first.'

Orson Beadle sat at the bar, sipping his Scotch.

'Sell a lot of that stuff?' the landlord said.

'It's a growth market,' Beadle said. 'That's where I work. Growth areas. Promotion, if you like.'

'I see, yes.'

Beadle looked across at the landlord. 'If you like — I can keep an eye on the bar, while you . . .'

'Oh no, that's quite all right.'

'I tell you what,' Beadle said, reaching into his jacket. 'I'll leave you a sample. Try it out, when you have a moment. See what you think. I can drop back for it.'

'If you're quite sure.'

'It's no problem,' Beadle said, placing a shiny black cardboard carton with a Perspex window on the bar. 'And that's a very good model.'

There was a howl from the gents' toilet. Beadle finished his drink.

'Another?' the landlord asked.

Beadle signalled him to fill it up.

The man who had run into the toilet was in the only cubicle. He had braced himself against the door, and was bent over, sweating. Someone started hammering on the door.

'I know you're doing something rotten in there,' the voice shouted out. 'Now hurry up and let me in.'

'Go away,' the man said. 'Go and watch the match.'

'I'll tear the fucking door off its hinges,' the man said, and began hammering again, more violently. 'I'm telling you I will. I'll tear the fucking thing down.'

'The there will be no cubicle. And you'll – be – back – to – square one. Ooooh! Be patient.'

'Christ,' the man said. 'You think I can wait?'

The man inside the cubicle heard a belt and a zip being

undone; the belt clattered to the floor as the trousers fell around the man's ankles.

'You think I can wait?' the man shouted out.

It was nearly closing time. Anyone passing the pub would have heard a buzzing sound, a low humming, coming from within; a steady, rhythmic whirring, the sound of men of action, the sound of men at work.

The sound was drowned out when an old grey box Cortina, the colour of paint primer, turned into the alleyway at the side of the pub and beeped its horn twice. It drove into the car park and pulled into a space, and the driver disembarked. He was a short man with sprouts of patchy hair, and he walked with a limp but he moved along the side of the car with distinct determination, his tongue lolling out of the side of his mouth.

Inside the pub, Beadle finished his drink and looked at his watch. Noting the time, he rapped his empty glass twice on the bar counter. The men in the bar looked round.

'Gentlemen,' he said, 'it is time.'

Beadle got down off his barstool. 'I can see you've all enjoyed yourselves.' The men murmured in agreement. 'Well then, that is good. But let us proceed.' Beadle headed over to the exit door to the car park. The men watched him go. As he got to the door, he turned and said, 'Follow me. Let us embark.'

The men zipped up and followed, carrying their things. The manager came out from behind the bar, locked the front doors, and went out after them.

As Beadle walked across the car park towards the Cortina, he noticed that it was rocking from side to side, the hatchback ajar, squeaking as it rocked up and down. Beadle approached, pulled the door open, and saw his assistant, Monteith, his trousers round his ankles, fumbling and fucking the very top-of-the-range, life-like, pump-and-fuck doll that Beadle was planning to demonstrate. Beadle reached and took one of the longer rubber dildos from one of the men standing behind him, and thwacked it across Monteith's undulating buttock cheeks. Monteith cried out, rolled off, and scrabbled out of the back of the car, pulling up his trousers. Beadle handed him the dildo and turned to the men.

'Now gentlemen, as you'll see, this is a top-of-the-range pump-and-fuck doll, with textured hair, squeezable, biteable tits that feel real and squirt milk, kneadable butt cheeks and tight holes, one hundred per cent bendable with elastic flesh and an articulated endoskeleton. I know, I know what you're going to say . . . that I said you wouldn't ever need another woman again. And that's true, I stand by that, but once in a while, gentlemen, you'll want company, and this is it. This is the world's finest love doll, *this* is the revolution. They come in all shapes and sizes, thin, fat, black, white, and they're all stacked, oh yes. Now, gentlemen, what I propose to do is allow you all, for a nominal fee, to try out the love doll. Correct me if I'm wrong, but after your moment of self-abuse in there, I am willing to bet that you all feel a little shameful and perhaps nauseous. Believe me, I'm feeling that just looking at you. What better way to release yourself from that mood than to have a go on this beautiful thing? It will put everything into perspective. Just leap on in and do as you please. It is quite resilient, the limbs bend every which way, you can bite it and hit it if you please and there'll be no complaints. Now gentlemen, form an orderly queue, and, of course, a nominal fee . . .'

Monteith relieved the first man of his cash and the man clambered in and set to work. Monteith assisted him by prodding his buttocks with the dildo. Soon a second man had clambered in. The crowd had started to shout encouragement and suggestions. Others crept off into the shadows with their sex toys and pleasured themselves until it was their turn.

'Steady gentlemen, one at a time,' Beadle said, helping Monteith push another man into the back. There were three or four of them in there by now. The crowd were getting unruly and shouting out obscenities. All the hair had come off the doll, the wig had been thrown out of the window, and one of the arms was coming loose.

'Bring the car round when you're finished,' Beadle

whispered to Monteith. Monteith nodded and got in the back with the other men.

Beadle walked across the car park casually, whistling to himself, his hand tapping the wad of money in his pocket.

As he turned into the alleyway, he heard Monteith call out, 'Don't that feel just like pubic hair?' sounding like he was choking on a furball.

the suicide kit

Worn out?

Lonely?

Depressed as hell?

Finding it tough even to read this?

Can't get a job? Can't find anyone to talk to? Past your sell-by date?

On some form of medication – floxotin, maybe phalypthromin – which you're too scared to come off in case the dark clouds return, which they will do and have done when you forget to take your tablet even for a single day?

Slipped so far down it feels like you'll never be able to come up again?

Can't face another sleepless night?

Can't face another day after another sleepless night?

Can't go on?

Then don't.

Start again.
    A new life.
    A new beginning.
    A totally fresh start.

How?
    With The Suicide Kit.
    With this fast, safe, proven-effective method of self-termination, you can leave this world behind and start again.
    Who knows what you'll be reborn as? Maybe the afterlife will offer you a better opportunity. If things don't work out, there's always The Suicide Kit again.
    Don't believe in the afterlife? Then what could be better than an eternity of blissful sleep?

Try The Suicide Kit.
    Because it's your life and your decision.

Friends and family — buy two kits, get one free.
    Ask about our 'buy now pay later' scheme.

www.suicidekit.com

As seen on *Why Me?*

acknowledgements

Thanks to:

Lesley Shaw, my agent, and David Milner, for their leap of faith; Stuart Williams at Secker; Bo Fowler; Danny O'Neill; Alex Hayles; Paul Hayles; Ma and Pa Hayles; Chay Hayles; Benny Weekes; Kieran O'Sullivan; Jonathan Gibbons; C. Pudsey; Laurie Hill; Glenn Barden; Louis Caulfield; Justin Moul; Will Gethin; Darren Bender; Todd Brooker; Vic Lambrusco; Sîon Brewell; Christian Ulmen; Luis Enrique Roman; Paolo Proto.